FIRE HEART

MAGIC AND MAGE SERIES EPISODE 2

ANGHARAD THOMPSON REES

FIRE HEART

*A*mara held the power of the world between her hands; the strength of raging oceans and the whisper of growing flowers both. With delicate fingers, the young witch condensed the power into a clear glowing orb—a sphere the color of tears that coalesced in her palms. A smile flickered at the corner of her lips and she clasped her hands together, hiding the magic from her watching sisters. Then, lowering her lips to her cupped hands, Amara incanted—drawing old words from old places. Blowing onto her fingertips, she opened them like a petal to the morning sun. And from her hands, flew a butterfly, its wings as blue as a robin's egg.

Her sister Fae delighted, reaching out for the butterfly as it fluttered around her golden hair. Her ice-blue eyes followed the creature as it looped and twirled and danced over the summer meadow.

"Better, Amara," said Mother, no delight in her voice. Just cool approval as her middle daughter cast. Fae, youngest, all spring air and happiness, nodded with mock seriousness before side-eyeing her sister.

"You have set a tough challenge, I will have to work hard to beat that!" said Fae, though the smile on her face conveyed that she already had something magical in mind.

"Wait," Amara said, middle sister, serious, dark and brooding. She raised an eyebrow. "I am yet to finish."

Amara lifted an elegant hand, the long sleeve of her ebony dress falling past her elbow to trail the soft grass below. The butterfly flew to her like a jaunty, happy tune, and alighted upon her fingers. At her touch it multiplied, two, three, six, a dozen butterflies of every color flourished around her, creating a gentle breeze of fluttering wings. By the time Amara turned to her mother to check her assessment, thousands of butter-flies danced in the quiet midday sun, and her mother's face exploded into a rare grin.

"Stupendous, Amara! That's my girl." She clapped her hands together like an excited child, and continued, her voice full of wonder. "That's my clever witch."

Amara took a deep bow like a master showman

completing his pièce de résistance and stepped aside for her youngest sister Fae to take her place on the stage of meadow grass and bluebells.

"No," Mother said, turning to Morganne, eldest sister. "You need to try."

Morganne sighed, turning away. "I've already tried, as you well know, and nothing happens—ever."

"Then try harder," Mother ordered, commanding Morganne with one angry finger. "Here. Now."

Morganne rose with a heavy sigh, tossing a knot of daisies she had been fumbling between her fingers, to the ground.

"Mother, there is little point. I have in common with my sisters nothing but the same birthdate. We may be triplets in blood, but not in magic. I don't know why you keep putting me through such torture."

"I do it for you to learn. Now, *try.*"

Morganne stared at her hands, her pale, pale hands adorned with freckles and hopelessness.

Breathe, she thought to herself, trying to center her focus. She closed her emerald eyes and imagined the power of nature coursing through her blood to her fingertips.

Yet she felt no change.

She willed magic to her palms, *please,* she begged in the quiet of her mind, but not an ounce of power rose from her blood to the surface of her skin. She stopped trying, but kept her eyes closed, not wanting to see the look of disappointment on her kin's faces.

"That's enough," Mother said, her voice laced with displeasure.

Morganne gulped, opening her eyes but diverting them from stares she could feel penetrating into her worthless, non-magical soul.

When she did glance up, Mother shook her head. Fae attempted a weak smile of condolence, and Amara turned away, embarrassed.

"As you were, Fae," Mother said, her voice stern with vexation. "Morganne, sit down and pay attention instead of fiddling with daisy chains or staring off into nothingness." Mother's attention turned back to Fae, opening her hands to welcome her youngest daughter to begin.

Fae, abashed by her eldest sister's reprimand, concentrated while the gentle river babbled alongside her; summer birds and busy wrens fluttered overhead, chasing Amara's butterflies away. But Morganne, eldest sister, *once* the voice of reason, did not stay to see what her other clever little sister could do. She did not stay to observe what her witch heart sister cast with magic and beauty and that old, old power. Instead, she rose from her cross-legged position, tied her unkempt, flowing red locks into a scruffy knot at the base of her neck, and walked barefoot toward home.

"Morganne!" Her mother called. *Demanded.* "Stay here. You may learn something from your younger siblings. Fae has such delicate accuracy with her casting, not as flamboyant as Amara perhaps, but her technique is faultless."

Morganne bit the words flaming in the back of her throat like wildfire and burning dreams. Morganne was powerless, and as her mother focused back to Fae, with an illusion surrounding her youngest sister of snowy mountain peaks and white skipping foxes shimmering under the midday sun, she realized she was not only powerless but pathetic too.

Nobody tried stopping her as she meandered home alone. Nobody even noticed she had gone.

2

HIDDEN MEANINGS

*M*organne peeked from behind the curtain, double and triple checking neither sisters nor Mother wandered toward home. She scoffed at the thought. *Why would they bother to come home?* They lost hours upon hours magic-making in that meadow, and Morganne felt she lost hours of her life there watching her special sisters perform—or rather, watching her mother's love for them grow. The only thing Morganne seemed capable of achieving was an increase in pity from her sisters and growing disappointment from her mother's eyes. Neither of which filled the gaping hole within her that ached to hold the elusiveness of her family bloodline.

Magic.

With this thought, Morganne bit a trembling lip that quivered with the same old symphony.

Why not me?

Morganne chided herself for such petulant thoughts. There had to be a way to discover magic, and she was sure the way rested in the book her mother allowed her sisters to read, but not her.

Breath held, she took tentative steps into her mother's bedroom, checking over her shoulder as the wooden door creaked behind her. Eyes wide, she tiptoed to the wooden chest at the bottom of her mother's bed. It was strangely ornate and out of place in their humble dwelling. Gold flourishes adorned each corner in decorative splashes, as if liquid gold solidified as it splashed, causing eruptions of cascading, golden waves. It looked like it came from another time, another world perhaps.

It must be worth a king's ransom, Morganne thought, stroking the huge golden keyhole at the center. She tested the lid, and though heavy, it opened without complaint. It was, of course, unlocked. Morganne sensed a twang of guilt in the hollow in her stomach that made her look over her shoulder again. Discovering the chest was unlocked, that her mother trusted her with such secrets, quickened Morganne's pulse all the more.

I shouldn't be doing this. Still, she heaved, opening the thick wooden trunk with a grunt.

A sudden thump on the ground beside her caused Morganne to gasp and let go of the lid. It *whomped* back down, sending wafts of old air and ancient magic into the darkening room.

"Oh!" Morganne said, her hand at her pumping heart. "It's you."

Shadow, the household cat, eyed her suspiciously and padded toward her, tail rigid and upright. He curled around Morganne, his black fur shining like obsidian stone as she petted him to calm her nerves. She went for the lid again, and the cat mewed; a short, sharp pitch of warning. Morganne shook her head at him.

"Oh, come on, I'm not stealing anything. I'm *looking*."

She ignored his whines and shooed him away when the cat clambered onto her lap. Morganne hoisted the lid for the second time and, checking over her shoulder for the third time, rummaged beneath the woolen blankets and bedclothes.

"I know it's here somewhere," she uttered, then her fingers found the leather spine. She did not need magic for its presence to shock her, causing her hand to retract for but a second. Her fingertips tingled for a moment…

with magic. She sighed. Magic was not something she could describe; magic was a *feeling*. As if the air became lighter, and light became brighter. Or like the sensation between dreaming and waking, those few short magical seconds of an entirely different reality, where time stands still and merges with infinite possibilities. This was the feeling she had now as her fingers grazed the leather tome.

Shadow wailed.

Morganne smiled, and the book within her hands moaned as she brought it into the candlelight.

"*The Cheval Book of Shadows,*" Morganne whispered, her fingers hovering over her surname.

Shadow skulked away, giving up his warning—giving up on Morganne. Cats are like that. He hopped onto the window frame and slithered through the open window, disappearing into the evening hue and leaving Morganne, eldest sister, once the voice of reason, with a burden she was yet to realize she carried.

Each page she turned seemed to sigh as if waking from a century-long sleep. The parchment yellowed and dog-eared, the ink faded to a light gray as she took in the illustrations, symbols, and ancient, ancient spells.

"This is magnificent," Morganne said, gulping down her awe and excitement. *Why has Mother not let me study from this book?* Possibilities surged around the hollow of her stomach, the desperate place where she yearned and ached for the magic—and the hope to bring her sisters back close.

She spoke as she read, "Dark Power Herbal and Plant Associations…" she screwed up her nose a little and continued turning the pages. "Consecration of the Dark Aspect Tool…"

She pulled a face without realizing and shook her head. "What are these spells? Ah—" She bent double over the book, her nose only inches from the age-old page that smelt of forgotten secrets. "Spell Casting and Bindings—The Ancient Rituals."

Flicking through the pages she smiled, there were spells for love, spells for beauty, spells for good health and wealth. The handwriting changed between spells and sometimes notes added by another hand appeared in the margins, presumably to enhance or improve them; like family recipes passed down from generation to generation.

Soon, the spells became darker, written in what once may have been a red ink, now faded to flesh pink. The handwriting grew unsteady and spidery; spells to uncover lies, spells for revenge. None of these interested Morganne. Urgency smothered her as she continued to search, no longer worrying she may tear or harm the fragile pages as she raced through the book.

"Where is it? There's got to be a spell here some-where to…" she gasped. "A Spell to Bind Magic. That's it! That's got to be it! I could bind magic to myself!"

Morganne let the book rest on her knees while she clasped her hands over her heart. She made a silent prayer and a whisper of a smile. Her fingers traced the title of the spell.

"Wait, oh no!" Her heart dropped several inches. "No, no… No!"

Below the title was a jagged line she had failed to see in her haste—a tear, right across the page, to expose the spell beneath for something else entirely. She flipped the tiny sliver of paper, exposing several more pages torn from the book.

The binding spell was gone.

"Morganne!" her mother's voice screamed; a mixture of dread and hurt and fear that sounded only like anger and hate. "What are you doing with my grimoire?"

In two strides, her mother was upon Morganne, ripping the book from her clutches. Morganne scram-bled to her feet, flustered.

"I'm sorry… I was—"

Mother struck her face, slapping the words of apology from her mouth with a piercing sting.

Mother and daughter stared at one another in

disbelief. Fae and Amara, rushing to the bedroom and the raised voices, covered their mouths in horror at the threshold.

"Oh dear child, I am sorry," Mother sobbed, throwing the book to her bed and pulling Morganne into a tight embrace. Morganne remained as rigid as stone beneath her mother's arms. "It's the book. It's a terrible book. And a very dangerous thing for those who don't know how to wield its power."

Morganne took three deep breaths, composing herself and willing her tears away before she spoke. "Then pray, why would you have such a thing? Why would you let my younger sisters read it and not I?"

Her mother pulled back, holding the top of Morganne's arms. She smiled, sympathetically, then flicked a glance to her magical daughters standing in the doorway. "Morganne," she began, "you don't possess magic, so I'm afraid it's something you will not understand."

The words stabbed at her heart.

"Oh, I understand. I understand *exactly*," Morganne spat, pulling away and striding from the room, the shape of her mother's hand flaming with rage and fury against her bruising cheek.

3

A LEAF FROM A BOOK

"I still cannot believe Mother hit you," Fae cooed, moving Morganne's flame red hair from her cheek to inspect the bruise.

"And neither can I believe you would rummage through her things like that," Amara added, a scowl between her thick black brows.

Morganne shot her a glare. "If it is such a terrible artefact, then why should Mother keep it in the house? Allow you to read from its pages?" she asked, but her guilt rose as anger, and her words were full of spite. "Besides, I thought grimoires were family heirlooms, notes passed on from generation to generation."

Amara softened then, a little. Her serious black eyes staring into darker thoughts. She paced the bedroom floor the three girls shared, feet muffled on the sheepskin rug. "Yes, you're right. And that's the big question, isn't it? Why is the book such a terrible thing, and why has she not warned Fae and I about its power?"

"And why are the pages and spells ripped from the book, like you mentioned?" Fae pondered.

Morganne's eyes narrowed. "You mean to say neither of you can tell, even with hearts full of magic?"

Amara blew out a breath in frustration. Fae took Morganne's hand. "Magic isn't a cure-all, dear sister. It cannot do all things, solve all problems."

"Well, it would solve mine!" Morganne despised the jealousy in her own voice. She shook her head. "I am sorry, sister, I do not mean to bite at you, either of you." She turned to Amara once more and attempted a half smile; but she still could not find it within herself to forgive her middle sister for lying to her, for making Morganne believe she had magic when she had none. "I just want us to be back the way we were, sisters of three."

"But of course we're still sisters," Amara said, as serious as thunder. Beside her, Fae nodded like a gentle breeze. Morganne turned away, sensing the pulsating magic within her sisters, making her own heart feel both heavy and empty in comparison.

"But it is not the same, is it? You spend so much time together casting and practicing your spells. And

Mother takes not one look at me anymore other than to chastise me or worse." She gestured to her bruised cheek. "I see the disappointment in her eyes—no, let me finish Amara—I see that same disappointment in your eyes, too."

Amara turned away then, unable to hold her stare, because like it or not, her sister spoke the truth. Silence engulfed them for several long heartbeats, so when Morganne spoke again, even though in a whisper, her words boomed in the darkening gloom.

"I would do anything for magic, absolutely anything," Morganne whispered.

A candle snuffed out on the windowsill.

"Do not say such a thing," Fae said, concern wrapped around every word. She clasped her sister's hand and shook her head, glancing at the candle from the corner of her eye. Blue smoke swirled from the wick, trailing toward them.

Amara said nothing, and instead, stared at the moon from the bedroom window. It was but a sliver in the dark sky—a slice of a wicked smile in the midnight hour. And she did not altogether trust the message it conveyed to her, but she repeated it all the same. "Perhaps there is something we can do to help you get magic, perhaps…" she trailed off, her blood pumping to the tune of *something is wrong;* it gnawed at her bones but her sister, her poor eldest sister stared back so hopelessly it was pitiful.

Fae bit her lip and backed away one cautious step.

"The spell you mentioned, the one missing from the book…" Amara began.

"The binding spell?" Morganne asked.

Amara nodded. "Perhaps we can summon the ripped pages. Perhaps we can cast to make them reappear."

Thunder roared in the distance, like an angry waterfall cascading into the depths. The night darkened, and the moon's wicked smile hid behind a grumbling cloud.

"I'm not sure about this," Fae said, fearing the growing winds that howled through the gaps in the windows. Several more candle flames flickered and threatened to extinguish.

"Why not?" asked Morganne, heart clanging against her ribcage. "After all, surely my magic will emerge someday. This will just make it happen sooner. Make us sisters again, in flesh and heart."

"We owe our eldest sister the chance," said Amara, though she knew in part this was only to ease her guilt for allowing her sister to believe she could perform magic. She opened both hands in a gesture for her sisters to join her, and they did.

Making a circle of three, Amara began. "Close your eyes, sisters, and imagine the pages of the book. Hold only that image in your mind."

Lightning crackled outside the window, illuminating the girls in their magic circle.

"Repeat after me." Amara opened one eye to check her sisters had closed their eyes then continued.

"By wind and air and fire and sea,

what once was lost

return to me,

I now invoke the law of three

to return the pages—mote it be…"

Thunder growled, rain pelted the window, and wind howled like a screaming child through the gaps of the crumbling wooden frame. The girls flung their eyes open, alert, breath short.

"What's happening?" Morganne asked, not hiding the quiver in her voice. Fae said nothing, but glared at Amara, jumping when another roar of thunder raged.

"Again," Amara called. The three girls repeated the words, shouting over the storm as it seethed in fury against the cottage.

Ahead of them, appearing at eye level, paper crinkled into life, forming a page. Spidery ink sprawled its way across the ancient parchment.

"You've done it!" Morganne shrieked, desperate to

hold the page in her hands, but her sisters held them fast, as the spell continued.

The bedroom door thundered open.

"No!" screamed Mother, her face contorted into fear and rage both, "No, no!"

She clapped her hands together, whispering old, old words from her trembling lips, and the paper burst into flames.

"Mother?!" screamed Morganne, dropping her sisters' hands.

"Do not break the circle!" Amara and Mother ordered in one terrified command.

But the window smashed open. Wind raged through Morganne's red hair like a furious flame. Books fell from their shelves. Curtains billowed.

Fae and Amara grabbed their sister's hands to recreate the circle.

"You need more power than that to stop what you started," Mother barked, forcing her way into the circle.

She grabbed Morganne's left hand and squeezed it with such force Morganne feared it would break.

Mother yelled into the storm. "Darkness leave us, leave, be gone! In our homes and hearts you don't belong!"

The ground trembled, but the storm receded,

taking with it the air from the sisters' lungs. Then in a heartbeat, it was over. Mother fell to the floor, gasping. The sisters shared fearful glances.

"You..." Mother began as she clambered to her feet. Her eyes brimmed with tears as she stared at Amara. "You almost released the Immortal One."

Amara blinked—twice. "*What?*"

"You have so much to learn and you're moving too fast to comprehend the dangers of magic." Mother stopped short and shook her head, long gray tresses agreeing with her disgust. She spat to the floor and the three sisters backed away. This was not how their mother reacted, to *anything*. "*She*, if you can call the evil being that, had her magic and title stripped from her eons ago, her spells cast out as she was. That's why the pages have been ripped and burnt from the book. Both she and her magic banished and spellbound to ensure the safety of witches and humanity."

"The Immortal One?" Morganne asked. "You've never mentioned such a being. Who is she?"

"I cannot say," their mother said as grave as death. "For even to speak her name may give her power. You must forget her, as we all have, and leave her memory to rot in the hole that imprisons her. You cannot play with fire, my daughters." She turned to Morganne. "Especially not you. Now please, go to bed, all of you.

We shall speak of this in the morning." She cast her eyes to the sly moon outside the broken window. "I do not trust that waning moon tonight."

And to bed the girls duly went, but one name played over in Morganne's mind. She had seen it on the page before the flames licked it to ashes.

Emrysa.

And it followed her into her sleep.

A CALLING

*M*organne knew she was dreaming by the way her mind flitted from one strange place to another with no connection, yet seamless all the same. And she knew she was looking for *something* as her eyes scanned the rooms and forests and mountains flickering across the canvas of her mind. A wind danced through the dreamtime air, the type of air that does not believe in gravity, leaving you free to fly or swim or twirl like a dervish. And Morganne did twirl, this way and that, desperately seeking *The Thing*.

But what *am I looking for?* She asked herself in a moment of clarity.

Morganne, a voice sang along the wind from both far away and close. As if it called from both epic mountains in the far distance and inside her own mind. *Morganne*, it called again, as sweet as summer apples. *I have what you seek.*

And at that moment, she became lucid. Not quite awake but not dreaming all the same, despite standing in a darkened valley under a shimmering blue moon, yet aware of the soft pillow beneath her head. A nighttime raven flitted past, its wing slicing through the air causing her red hair to dance like fall's leaves around her face. The sensation of the pillow beneath her head disappeared completely.

And she knew.

She was searching for her dream, for what she desired most in her waking life.

Magic.

Where are you? Morganne asked, twirling again. Images flashed through her mind's eye. A mountain pass, a craggy old rock shaped like a rearing horse, a stream running with violet water.

*Find me…*the sweet voice whispered and Morganne knew if she answered the call, she would bind herself to a promise. An oath.

*Find me…*it sang again like gentle lullabies and calming fireside warmth.

Morganne nodded and looked at the full blue moon.

I will. I will find you, Emrysa.

Morganne's eyes snapped open.

She was asleep no more.

TO BELONG

"What was I thinking?" Morganne chastised herself. She splashed cool river water on her face. The sun was barely up, but she could not sleep, not after that dream. So she had dressed and donned her cloak and padded along the dew-stained grass toward the river, the cool morning touch cleansing away the guilt crawling upon her skin.

She stared at her reflection a little while, shaking her head at the memory of her vivid dream.

It was just a dream. Behind her, Angelfire's familiar hoof beats swished through the long grass toward her.

"Hello, boy," she said, rising and patting his sleek neck, his skin warm beneath her palm. He blew the soft blow belonging only to gentle horses; a sound of contentment and peace, and though Morganne could not speak with the horses like her witch sisters, she understood Angelfire's meaning all the same. The chestnut horse stepped closer, resting his long head into her body—his mane of fire tumbling down to his knees, and she hugged him. Her red locks getting lost in his.

"Thank you for being here for me," she said into his musky-smelling coat. "These days, I would be all alone if it were not for you. I just wish I had the ability to speak with you as my sisters can."

Angelfire whickered.

Find me…

Morganne gasped, and for a fraction of a heart-beat, she wondered if the voice came from Angelfire. He stamped a hoof, which she took to be a denial, and pinched the sensitive skin on the underside of her arm to prove she was no longer asleep. No, this was not a dream, and the voice was as real and as solid as the horse standing beside her. Something pulled at the hollow in her stomach, the longing, the aching for magic. To be like her sisters: in flesh and heart. Her dreams, the voice, her desires—they all coalesced. And she knew.

The voice was real.

"Why should I seek you?" Morganne asked the sky, her guilt forcing anger from her trembling lips.

Angelfire stepped back, tossing his head. His mane danced like flames.

She waited.

Nothing. Just the predawn preparations of shuffling birds and burrowing insects. Angelfire resumed chomping on the meadow grass and Morganne laughed at herself, wondering perhaps if she was still half asleep and half dreaming.

You will seek me, now or later Fireheart, for I have what you desire. No other witch is strong enough to pull out your magic from within than I.

"Fireheart?" Morganne repeated aloud, tasting the name on her lips, and feeling the flames in her heart ignite with the idea that perhaps she had magic stuck within. And if so, the words had credence. Had her mother not failed to awaken Morganne's magic, as had her sisters? She knew her mother feared this witch, had pushed her to strike Morganne's face in a manner so uncharacteristic. But still, if this immortal witch could do as she promised, would the risk of awakening her from her spellbound state be worth it?

I would do anything for magic, Morganne recalled saying to her youngest sister, Fae. She gathered her resolve.

"If I find you, do you promise to grant me magic? Will I command nature the way my sisters cast?"

A laugh, not sinister, but serious all the same, danced along a passing cloud.

Find me, and I will make you more powerful than all…

Morganne sucked air between clenched teeth. It wasn't power she wanted. She wanted to be like her sisters.

But I will be *the eldest sister again, they may respect me once more instead of dismissing every word I say,* Morganne pondered, justifying what she already knew deep down was wrong.

With conflicting mind and heart both, Morganne led Angelfire to the stable block, wondering all the while if he could understand her inner monolog.

I shouldn't be doing this. I should wait for Mother to explain more about this witch as she promised last night. But why should I care what Mother believes? She cares so little about me and my feelings. And what of my sisters? They won't care, will they? They'll just go back to casting in the pretty meadow while I'm left to tend the fire and hearth like a poor scullery maid in a badly written fairytale.

Her thoughts looped, around and around, justifications and ramifications both. Yet, she had already decided.

With haste, Morganne saddled Angelfire, her trembling fingers fumbling with the black leather straps of the bridle and girth. Angelfire stomped a hoof, swished a tail, and Morganne did not need a witch heart to know he was just as agitated as she.

"It's okay, boy," she lied, more to calm herself than to calm the horse. "I'm sure everything will be fine… just a little trip, a little journey. A little *voyage*." She giggled—a nervous, theatrical performance—knowing she was fooling no one, not even herself.

Overhead, a raven cawed, and Morganne tried to ignore its warning as she ran to the kitchen to fetch provisions for her saddlebag.

Should I leave a note?

Soft snores drifted from her bedroom, and she tiptoed to the door to peek at her sleeping sisters. *I'll be back before sunset. No need to alarm them with my notes and motives.* She closed the bedroom door and trotted back to the stables.

Within moments, Morganne put her left toe in the stirrup and swung herself up into Angelfire's saddle, grasping the reins as if some part of her tried to stop herself from taking the journey forward. She took one last look over her shoulder at her safe little cottage where her sisters slept. *Magically.*

That thought clenched around her heart, and her face pinched in determination.

"Yah!" Morganne yelled, squeezing Angelfire's sides and flinging the reins forward to give the horse the freedom of his head. The fire-horse beneath her took off at a raging gallop; his thrumming hoof beats matching the erratic rhythm of the nerves stampeding in her stomach.

Emrysa, she thought, *I'm coming to find you.* A voice in her mind shrieked with laughter, no longer sweet and warm, but wild and enraged. Thunder bellowed across the sky as Angelfire flew like wildfire—crackling lightning following in their wake. But no, not following.

Chasing.

THE WEST WINDS

$\mathcal{M}$organne screamed as she turned her head. Lightning raced toward them, faster than the horse's pounding hooves covered ground. Crackling static rippled on Morganne's hair and skin, pushing her heart with its electrical current. And something else. A pulling sensation, as if the core of the universe pulled at her innards to join the roots of the world's trees, twisting and turning beneath the surface of the land.

Your oath, Emrysa said in her mind with all the fire of molten lava.

And Morganne knew in making her decision she had sealed the oath, and now it pulled at her.

"What have I done?" she sobbed. Tears streamed across her cheeks as they galloped head-on into the wind. The lightning reached out with tendrils—hooks of fire and light grappling for the girl. Angelfire galloped faster, Morganne low and light in the saddle as the horse's body rocked beneath her.

"We can't outrun it," she said through gritted teeth.

It caught her in a flash of blue flames.

Morganne flung her head back, her mouth wide open to scream, but no sound released. Instead, fire the color of the ocean's tears pooled from her mouth. It morphed, changing shapes, a raven's amber eye, a hilt of a sword, hands as old as time itself clasped around her slender neck. But Morganne saw these as abstract, fractured thoughts—almost blind with pain and heat and guilt. Angelfire reared, thrashing his rider from his back; but he did not gallop away. He watched, eyes bulging, blowing hard from widened nostrils as Morganne convulsed on the ground, shimmering with an otherworldly flame. He shrieked high into the sky, hoping it would carry on the winds to his companions, Shadowind and Moonglow, who he'd left grazing in the fields behind him. And though they heard it, they did not come.

They, too, were bound by flame.

Morganne whimpered as the last of the flames dissipated into the smoky air. The flame had scorched neither skin nor hair, but her heart still seethed with a blistering pain.

"I shouldn't have done this," she cried out as she scrambled on all fours and then to her feet, swaying with nausea. Angelfire tossed his red head and snorted; it would take more than Morganne's soothing hands to calm him.

"We've got to get back," she said, swinging into the saddle.

You cannot deny me nor change your mind. You made an oath, Fireheart.

Morganne gritted her teeth and fought the voice, but it was no good. The closer they galloped to the homestead, the louder the voice became.

You brought me to your home when you broke your magic circle. Now my presence can use the link as a touchstone.

"Then I shall break the link," Morganne cried over galloping hooves, her worry for her mother and sisters rising. But at least her family had magic. They might forever hate her for what she had done, but she would explain herself after they got rid of the black curse.

A sinister laugh in her mind only increased her panic.

You will not break the link.

A threat.

Angelfire rounded the corner and slammed into a standstill. He reared, screaming, into the smoky air.

"No!" Morganne whispered, clasping around the horse's neck to keep herself in place. She watched her house alight with cold, blue flame. Fae and Amara pounded the panes of the kitchen windows with all their might.

"Magic, why don't they use their magic to get out?" Morganne panicked.

I have spellbound them under my flame, said the cool voice as Morganne scanned the other windows for her mother. She found her. She was crying. Morganne had *never* seen her mother cry. From the window, her mother pressed her hands together in prayer, another first, and then waved a sad goodbye.

Angelfire pawed the ground, and Morganne noticed for the first time, Shadowind and Moonglow frozen in the same terrifying, life-sucking flames.

"Stop, please stop!" she begged, knowing the terror caused by this old, old magic, and the cruel memories it pulsed through her body while it had held her as its kindling.

The further you go from the touchstone, the less I can contact you. I need to be sure you will not change your fleeting mind. I need to be sure you would come for me as you promised—no matter what.

Her sisters pounded the windows still, their mouths wide open with screams and words that Morganne could not understand. The flames crackled up the cottage walls, engulfing it and the thatched roof.

"You tricked me!" Morganne screamed.

You awoke me, the voice snarled.

And Morganne thought back, back to the magic circle. Did not Amara specify to only think of the pages when she cast the spell? Was that all she had thought about? She bit her lip, knowing. No, she had wondered who the writer of the spell could be, and what powers the spells could wield. The witch was truth-telling. Morganne had awoken the Immortal One from her spellbound slumber. This was all Morganne's fault.

She suppressed an enraged scream and locked eyes with Amara through the window, whose cool composure diminished into panic and alarm... just like Morganne's own hope.

A flash of indigo, a bolt of lightning, thunder charged across the skies deafening the heavens and ripping light from the world.

Find me, free me from my curse, and then I shall be untethered from this place... and your family.

It felt like a half-truth.

The windows smashed, glass shattering like broken

dreams, and her sister's screams pelted toward her. Her mother yelled, "Run, Morganne! Run!"

Morganne shook her head. *No, I can't leave you.*

Oh, but you will, the voice said, amusement wrapping around the words. And within a breath, the blue flames engulfed her sisters and mother, embracing them in its cold terror of fears and bad dreams. *They will die within the next moon cycle if you do not release me. So listen, and listen closely.*

And she did, with terror, knowing there was only one way to save her family. But that meant releasing the cursed witch into the world, and who knew what terrible things she could achieve when her full power returned.

Morganne's heart thudded with her impossible choice. Leave her family to die, or risk the fate of the entire world to the Immortal One's whims.

"I shall do it!" Morganne called, hatred and guilt oozing from every word. "I shall release you."

You'll do more than that, said the voice in a cruel, taunting tone.

And Morganne turned Angelfire to the west winds and galloped into the unknown.

THE HILT OF A SWORD

*D*ays and nights passed in a blur of sour thoughts and crippling fear, and now, several days on, desperate hunger added itself to a cacophony of complaints. Morganne checked her saddlebag again, just in case, but not a morsel of her already sparse rations remained. She had even eaten the crumbs in the corner of the saddlebag, complete with hair and dirt and dust that also gathered there.

"It's all right for you," she said to Angelfire. "At least you can eat grass, there's plenty of that."

But it wasn't okay for Angelfire, not that he could tell her such things. The horse's heart felt as drained and as pained as her own. And if the thoughts of his friends and comrades locked in the blue flame were not enough, his entire body ached from the relentless pace at which they had covered ground to seek answers… or to ask bigger questions. But now they walked, both lacking the energy to push onwards. They wove their way through the thickening forests and waning paths like lost souls.

"What was that?" Morganne asked, pulling Angelfire to a standstill. The snapping branches under-hoof ceased. Silence. And Morganne blessed that beautiful sound—for it meant that Emrysa no longer had the ability to penetrate her mind. The further they moved from the touchstone that was Morganne's home, the fainter the Immortal One's voice became. Although in truth, it was a blessing and curse both, for how was she to find this witch cast into the unknown without that taunting voice to guide her? All Morganne had was the three visions from her blue-flamed torture and cryptic whispers from a voice in her mind that made no sense at all.

There it was again. A clang, a clatter. Metal on metal.

Bandits? Morganne shuddered. She wouldn't allow herself to get caught—not this time.

"Surrender," a cry demanded. Another clink of metal.

"Never!" yelled another.

Morganne squeezed Angelfire's side, encouraging him forward, and peered through the trees.

A flash of red and gold, a swirl of a cape. Shafts of evening light broke through the forest canopy, illuminating two young men in chain mail as they fought. She gasped, heart racing, and not *just* because of the brutal swordplay. She dismounted and tiptoed through the trees, pulling branches away to get a better look.

"You will surrender or die," the first called again, as he swung his sword downwards, both hands gripping the hilt. *One of the visions.* The powerful movement caught the second fighter by surprise, and his sword fumbled from his grasp to the forest loam. "Ah! Now you *must* surrender, Bedivere."

Bedivere, Morganne silently repeated, feeling the taste of the name in her mind.

But Bedivere did not surrender. In a movement so quick, Morganne could hardly keep up, he spun away from the sword and toward a tree, ripping a large branch off in one swift move. Then, like a dance, the dark-haired fighter, stepped—light and confident—toward the sword-bearer, all the while the branch twisted and turned hand over wrist, whipping the air with its speed.

"I may not have a sword, but I have fury, Kay!"

bellowed Bedivere as he swung the leafy weapon at his foe.

Kay, fair-haired with sharp features that somehow reminded Morganne of a fox, almost laughed. "You do not have fury, you moron. You have a twig," and he sliced upward in a lazy one-handed swing, chopping through the branch as if it were nothing more than kindling. Morganne's heart beat faster. She couldn't peel her eyes away from the fight… away from the dark-haired and dark-skinned boy. *Bedivere,* she repeated. Her fingers shot to her lips as he stumbled backwards, falling to the floor.

I should run. She knew better than to get involved in a fight like this, who knew what would happen if they realized she was there. *I should run…*but she watched the sun glint on the sharp blade poised for a killing blow, and further forward she stepped.

"Surrender or die," Kay threatened again, all humor replaced with a promise. He aimed the blade at Bedivere sprawled on his back on the ground. Morganne looked away, she had never seen a man killed before but… she looked back, back at Bedivere's stoic eyes staring at his killer without fear. Kay stepped forward again, the point of his blade pin-pricking the boy's neck.

Oh surrender, you fool! Morganne, breathless, noticed a dot of red forming around the point of the blade.

"Never," the stupid boy confirmed, and Morganne took a deep breath, cursing both the boy and herself.

"Stop!" she screamed, jumping from behind the trees and Kay turned, pointing the sword directly at her heart.

8

A LOW BLOW

"What on Arthur's crown?" Kay said, staring at Morganne. He looked back, incredulous, at the boy on the floor, dropped his sword and *smiled*—his face less sharp when his lips parted as wide as they did, squishing his blue eyes closed. "You know, convincing beautiful young maidens to save your life is not only cheating, Bedivere, but it's also some low cunning."

He bent down, offering a hand to Bedivere who accepted it with a sheepish grin that almost took Morganne's breath away. The boys embraced, the gesture familiar despite the awkwardness caused by their chain mail and gauntleted hands.

Morganne scowled, looking at both boys in turn, her eyes lingering just a little longer on Bedivere. "I thought you were fighting to the death?!" she said, angered and exposed.

Kay laughed and Bedivere dug him in the ribs with his elbow.

"What?" Kay asked, shrugging.

Bedivere shook his head. "I apologize for my half-witted friend here laughing at you," he said, stepping forward and removing his gauntlet to take Morganne's hand. "Let me introduce myself. I am—"

"A fool!" Morganne interrupted with such force he stepped backwards. "If that were a real fight, if you were not playing your silly sparring games, your pride and refusal to surrender would have got you killed!"

"But—"

"No buts, and then *I* probably would have got killed trying to stop *you* from getting killed, when I can manage getting killed all by myself, thank you very much."

"But—" Bedivere half laughed and turned to Kay with an incredulous shrug.

"And no, I will not accept your apology, before you waste your breath. And neither you," she cast her eyes at Kay whose face looked like it would split in two from the smile that continued expanding. "Nor *you*, shall stop me, or question me, or even look at me as I continue on my way. Thank you, and good day!"

She stopped, taking a much-needed breath, and smoothed down her cloak—as if that made the matter final. Her cheeks stung with heat as her embarrassment spread across her face, made worse by the two warriors staring at her in utter disbelief and, even worse, amusement.

Bedivere put both hands up in supplication and turned to Kay before continuing. "I'll take your sword fight any day over this maiden's sharp tongue. I fear the blade of her words could slice me into ribbons far quicker than your steel." And though he addressed Kay, he did not take his eyes from Morganne.

"Ah, my friend," Kay began, mirth brimming from his smile. "I fear she has already dealt a fatal wound to your heart by the way your doleful eyes pine at her."

"That's a low blow, Kay." Bedivere smirked.

"So too was attacking me with your twig of doom!"

Morganne turned on her heel, shaking her head as the boys continued sparring, this time with their witless words.

"Come on, Angelfire," she said, gathering the reins and swinging up into the saddle. "We have no time for this."

They had walked several paces before the warriors noticed and stopped squabbling.

"Wait!" cried Bedivere. "I'm afraid, no matter your

warning, we cannot let a young maiden travel the thick of the woods alone. We will accompany you on your journey. Where are you going?"

"I am not telling you," Morganne said, not even turning her head to address him, though it took all her restraint.

"Well then, in that case we shall follow until you reach your destination safe and sound. Kay, fetch the horses."

From behind, Bedivere's quick footsteps crunched on forest loam and dead leaves to catch up with her. Angelfire spooked, shuffling forwards, but Bedivere caught up, grabbing the reins and stopping them both. She looked down at him, and he half smiled. "Look, there are bandits and even worse out here. These are dangerous times—you know, several innocent young maidens, like your beautiful self, were recently captured and trialed as witches. Killed! For nothing more than a few golden coins. We are out here protecting young helpless damsels like yourself."

Morganne's jaw slackened. "*Helpless damsels?*"

He smiled, as if to confirm her words and to comfort her in the truth of it. Perhaps even awaiting her admiration. But Morganne shook her head, gritted her teeth, and kicked her foot forward in her stirrup, smashing Bedivere in the face with a cold metal twang and knocking him out in an instant. He fell to the floor with a thump and a slow clap commenced behind her.

"That is quite something. You know, usually, it's young maidens who faint and pass out to the floor in front of his magnificent good looks, not the other way around." Kay laughed, though his face betrayed a flickering emotion he tried hard to suppress. "He'll never live this down. Quite the ladies' man is our Bedivere… within the realms of Camelot at least."

"Yes, well not in my realm, thank you very much. And you'll find the only protection I need from you, or he, is to ensure that your witlessness does not contaminate me."

Kay said nothing, and just smiled a ridiculously large smile. He flicked a lock of golden hair from his eyes and raised an eyebrow, daring her to continue before he turned and picked his fallen comrade from the floor and flung him over a magnificent white steed.

Morganne huffed aloud and turned Angelfire away. "Good day," she called over her shoulder.

"Tut, tut, tut," Kay replied in a heartbeat, now sitting on the majestic white horse, several hands taller than Angelfire. "You *do* know it is a criminal offense to assault the king's men, madam?"

Morganne rolled her eyes, and Kay smiled with

mischief. "So it's off to the Camelot Court for you, Missy."

"Oh dear goddess," she cursed as Kay lassoed a rope that flung over her torso, locking her arms close to her body.

He tugged on the rope. "Here, kitty, kitty!" he cooed, pulling her along like a dog on a lead, and whistling out of tune as if he were enjoying a perfectly normal country ride.

9

AN AMBER EYE

*E*vening spread its darkness like a cloak across the land, and though pockets of light filtered through trees here and there, the forest succumbed to the night.

"We won't make Camelot for another day, at least," Kay said, breaking the hour-long silence that had passed. Morganne had long given up her useless cries of protest and avoided Bedivere's ice-cold stare at all costs—much to Kay's amusement. He shook his head, chuckling to himself as he watched Morganne and Bedivere strain to ignore one another as they rode side-by-side. "There's a clearing ahead," Kay said. "We should stop for rest and food."

The king's men dismounted and Morganne struggled to do the same with her arms bound.

"Here, let me," Bedivere said with a scowl as he reached for the knot in the thick rope. He paused, "I'm assuming you are not stupid enough to run off into the night if I untie you."

Morganne scowled, and Bedivere loosened the ropes, avoiding her gaze. His fingers brushed against her own, slowing to a stop. She gulped, blush rising to her cheeks, and she dared a glance into his deep black eyes. Her heart pounded, a stirring like magic in the hollow of her stomach. Then he turned away, breaking the spell, and Morganne chastised herself for allowing such thoughts to pass the canvas of her mind while her family suffered under the Immortal One's blue flame.

"I'm going to hunt for supper," Bedivere said as he stalked away, and Morganne's stomach clawed at itself and she salivated at the thought of eating. So when the warriors set up camp, complete with rabbits cooking on a crackling campfire, she clutched her hollow stomach and rocked at the painful aroma caused by fresh meat sizzling.

Eventually, Bedivere went about carving the meat with his gold-gilded dagger before handing a crispy skinned leg to Morganne. She snatched it from him, pausing for a heartbeat as the flames highlighted his bruised face. A deep purple stain crawled across his cheek and Morganne turned away with the guilt. But with hunger far outweighing her pity, she tore at the meat with her teeth and a ravenous fury, hardly chewing before swallowing the food down in hungry gulps.

"That's a heck of an appetite for a young maiden," Kay said, arching an eyebrow. He stopped chewing and watched, half in awe and half in disgust. He laughed lightly as he tucked into his own meager rations, talking with his mouth full. "Seen better table manners from the breeding sow! Haven't you?"

Kay turned to Bedivere, who had not much been in the mood for conversation since he woke up to find himself slung sideways upon his horse, and a headache to match any ale-made stupor. So instead, Bedivere ignored Kay and watched Morganne devour her food with caution and anger both.

"How long have you been on the road?" Bedivere asked. No more humor. No more lightheartedness or doleful eyes.

She shrugged, and ripped another mouthful of meat from the bone. "Days..." she said between chews. "Three, maybe four."

"Where are you going?" Bedivere's question more an interrogation.

She held his cold stare, and shrugged again. "I've already told you, I don't know."

Bedivere stood, looming over her like a tower. "Where. Are. You. Going?" he demanded; his hand reached for the hilt of his sword.

Morganne stopped chewing, and Kay shot up, placing his own hand over Bedivere's sword-clutched fist.

"Arthur's arse, Bedivere," he said, incredulous. "Stand down, for goodness' sake. You'll give me indigestion."

But Bedivere would not. "I will not stand down until this maiden tells us who she is and what she's doing. Who are you?" His hand grappled the sword in a tighter hold, his knuckles turning white.

"It matters not who am I, but what I am doing here. I am trying to save my family, and I will tell you again for the umpteenth time since you bound me, you *must* let me go—"

"Or what?" Bedivere said.

They stared at each other, seething, until rattling wheels and hoof beats sounded toward them. "What now?" Bedivere growled.

His eyes left her own, and Morganne realized she had been holding her breath. Bedivere stalked away from her into the darkness beyond the firelight to investigate.

Kay placed a hand on Morganne's shoulder. His

sharp features pinching though his blue eyes still glinted. "Sorry about that," he jerked his head several times in Bedivere's direction. "He can be an idiot some-times, but mostly you'll find he's great… at least, a great idiot. And about the sword thing, I don't think he would have killed you…" he smiled, "… much."

And despite herself, Morganne laughed along with him.

"Who goes there?" Bedivere called into the dark-ness ahead of them and the hoof beats, the creaking wood of a cart, and the whirl of wheels halted beside him. In the same moment, Morganne felt a pull at the deepest part of her soul, a clawing around the edges as if a raven's talons tried to strip her soul away.

Her oath stirred.

She paled, sweat rising to her temples and the merest of whispers filled her mind.

Closer, it said like a ghost of a thought, disappearing before the words fully formed. And Morganne was compelled to follow the sound of the voice that now croaked into the night upon a rotten cart.

"I am but an old gypsy traveler," a voice older than the forest rasped.

Morganne joined Bedivere's side, and he cast her an angry look, side-stepping away. The old woman pulled her hood down and erupted into a wheezing laugh that morphed into a coughing fit.

"Yes, you are right to fear her," the old woman said, glancing at Bedivere, then fixing a heavy stare at Morganne.

"You know of her?" Bedivere spat, hand clutching his sword once more.

"Oh," the hag wheezed. "I say this only for her beauty. With those flame locks and fire heart, her romance would be a difficult blaze to control."

Morganne flinched at the word and repeated it in her mind. *Fireheart.*

Kay wandered toward them, unaware of the brewing tension. "Greetings," he said, then jerked backwards, his face a comical grimace. He stared at the haggard old woman, her face pitted like ancient bark from a tree, and her eyes as dark as death itself. He cleared his throat, turning to Bedivere with a sly smile. "Your luck is in. Seems to be the day for *maidens* running astray unguided. Would you care to warm your bones at our fire, old woman?"

She nodded, but looked not at Kay, and instead, fixed those beady dark eyes on Morganne.

A crow cawed into the darkened sky.

"Don't mind him," the hag said, flicking age-old hands toward the back of the cart. Several cages trapping crows and ravens sat stacked amongst other covered boxes, and Morganne did not care to think what they concealed. A raven's amber eye watched her, it cawed again in time to the same scraping sensation within her bones. She gulped, remembering the blue flamed visions.

"Help an old woman down to warm her soul by the fire, would you?" she asked Morganne, proffering her hand adorned with age spots and blue, blue veins.

Morganne took it. Angelfire, grazing nearby, pawed the ground—agitated. Several crows sang sadness into the air.

"I have something for you, a message," the old woman whispered to Morganne as Kay and Bedivere set about cooking broth with the left-over meat and bones. The woman pulled at her cloak, exposing her collarbone that bore a darkened mark. Two black crescent moons back-to-back.

Morganne shrugged, nervous. "I—I don't know it's meaning."

And the old woman laughed a terrible laugh. "Oh child, you soon will. You soon will."

10

A PILE OF EARTH

*I*t did not take long before the king's men fell asleep, serenading the nighttime frogs and crickets with heavy snores. Morganne could wish for no such thing. She glared at the old hag across the fire's dying flames.

"She sent you?" Morganne asked, and the hag smiled, exposing her blackened gums like freshly dug graves.

"Nobody sent me, Fireheart. I am but a gypsy traveler. But I felt what you did, we all did." She pulled at her collar once more exposing the crescent moons as if that gave an answer to everything.

Bedivere snorted and rolled over. Morganne jumped in surprise, then watched him a few careful moments as the flames danced across his bruised face.

She softened then, watching the curl of his eyelashes and the fullness of his lips as he slept.

"How—How did you—and who is *we*?"

The hag glared.

"Tell me," Morganne demanded through gritted teeth, checking Bedivere had not stirred.

This time the hag smiled. "You awoke her, brought her memory back to life and invited her into your home —"

"I did no such thing!" Morganne spat, yet guilt pulsed through her veins. She closed her eyes to the truth, then softened her voice. "It was a mistake. You must understand it was all a stupid mistake. Please, I beg you..." Morganne reached out, taking hold of the old woman's arm. The hag pulled away, scowling. "Please, if you have any information that can help my family, then pray, you must tell me, I want nothing more than for this stupid quest to be over—"

"Over?" the old woman interrupted. "This will never be over. This is a war as old as time itself."

"What war?"

"Witches versus necromancers." The hag cackled, with an incredulous shake of her head.

Bedivere gasped, then imitated a few gentle snores. Morganne turned to him, but missed his eyes flinging open in surprise… in terror. He squeezed them shut now, laying as quiet as sleep itself as they continued, hoping to gain the information he knew they would not share had they known he was listening.

"I am no witch, old woman," Morganne spat when she was content the boy would not hear, her eyes narrowed in caution.

"And yet, here you are on a quest to unleash Emrysa herself! Queen of dark magic."

The words hit Morganne like a punch in her solar plexus. "My family is under her curse, what choice am I left with? Let my entire family die?"

The old woman nodded. "But I wonder what caused her the ability to latch onto them in the first place, child?" Her eyes narrowed, and Morganne understood that this hag did not wonder—she knew. "You must have welcomed her into your home, no? Greed, perhaps? Jealousy? Ah, yes, these are emotions Emrysa adores."

Tears stung the back of Morganne's eyes, and her nose tickled in a way it often did before crying. "Yes," Morganne admitted, gulping her tears away. "All of those things."

"You need not explain, child. You cannot wield the power like your sisters that much is clear. But you still have witch blood." The old woman picked at her grubby nails, feigning nonchalance or indifference, but

Morganne sensed the hag's hunger from across the fire. A shadow flickered across the old woman's face. "Are you not aware that spells do not need magic to work, no?"

Morganne's green eyes widened, but she remained silent, waiting for the hag to continue. And she did.

"A spell," she said, snarling up her face as if a bad smell had floated by. "A spell is nothing more than a recipe. Just as you can bake a cake by following simple instructions, so you can create a spell. Say the right words, use the right tools. It's all—" her nostrils flared with distaste. "—Academic."

"You mean to say I don't need magic to find Emrysa?"

The old woman shook her head, and a smile crept across her paper-thin skin as though it would slice her face apart. "That is correct. Spells and magic are different. A spell created by a witch is a recipe, a set of instructions that work with nature. Magic is a magnificent manipulator. It takes nature, and bends it to a whim, it's a fantastic and cruel power… in the wrong hands."

And as if testing her own words, the old woman rubbed her own decaying hands together until a miniature thunderstorm formed in her palm—a foreboding black cloud filled with minute lightning and power pulsing in the dark.

"Tell me," Morganne said, edging closer to the old witch. "Tell me how I can find her and reverse this stupid mistake."

"Rather you than me, Fireheart—for though I wish to see Emrysa returned to this world in flesh and blood, I would not want to pay the price to be the one to do so."

"If I do not find her, I'll pay with a heavier price. What can be worth more than my mother and sisters' lives?" Morganne's voice rose, and she winced at herself, checking the bulk of both Kay and Bedivere's sleeping bodies once again.

"Come, help up my old bones." The woman gestured from the small log she sat upon. Morganne sighed and helped the hag rise, noticing the touch of the woman's hands were as cold as ice, despite the warmth of the fire. "Do as I say, though I shall not incant or be any part of this. Now, draw a circle, a large circle here in the open, and place a pile of earth just there."

Morganne trailed a circle with the toe of her boot in the forest loam, and scrambled together the pile of earth, her fingertips black and dry.

"Opposite it, you need water," the witch continued

and Morganne picked up the water skin lying next to Kay and placed it in the circle. "Good, good. Now, fire is easy, you can get a small flame a'flickering from the campfire, no?"

Morganne did, scalding her fingers in the process.

"Now, you need a representation of air. As you might have already guessed, the four elements of this world will complete your magic circle."

Both Morganne and the witch looked around for inspiration. "We did not do this at home," Morganne muttered, knowing air to be as impossible to catch as wishes.

"No, because your sisters used magic." The hag cackled, her cruel words twisting like a knife in Morganne's side.

Morganne forced a heavy exhale, stopping mid-breath.

"Oh!" Morganne thought with sudden clarity. "Breath." She knelt and blew on the circle boundary with a long, slow exhale.

"Yes, yes," cooed the old witch.

In the darkness of the shadows, several ravens cawed. A hard shove sent Morganne stumbling backwards into the circle.

"Get in there," the witch ordered, her face darker than before and for several heartbeats, Morganne wondered if this was all a cruel trick. But what other choice did she have? Do nothing and her family would die. Try the spell and risk restarting an ancient war.

And all the while, unbeknown to her, Bedivere watched through his eyelashes, too stunned to stop what he knew he should.

"Walk the circle clockwise and repeat my words... carefully.

I call upon the goddess of night

To give me the power of second sight

To walk the path to where you stay

To find you by the break of day."

Morganne shuddered. The words, they sounded all wrong. Dark and heavy like death and dread. *I shouldn't do this,* she thought, the little voice inside that is not so much magic, but somehow always right. She could still hear her sisters' screams scraping at her bones. The final goodbye her mother gave, expecting to die. No, she was their only hope, and she would make this wrong right, somehow.

She walked the circle thrice, then stood, head cast back to the withering moon, hands splayed at her side. And she spoke the words.

"I call upon the goddess of the night..."

Wind howled through the midnight trees.

"To give me the power of second sight..."

Nothing. Not yet.

"To walk the path to where you stay…"

The flap of ravens' wings; a cackle of an old witch hoping for other things.

"To find you by the break of day."

The wind ceased. Still. Too still. Morganne looked around. Nothing had outwardly changed, save for Bedivere who sat bolt upright staring at her with those dark eyes that made her melt.

"What just happened?" he said, slowly rising to his feet, his cape askew.

Morganne stuttered, failing to find the words. Yes, she felt it too. Something.

Something.

He walked to her, alarmed, fearful, uncertain, and he held out his hands for her to go to him, his forehead creased with concern.

It's nothing, Morganne thought. Just the fear that accompanies expectation. She sighed, smiled at Bedivere, and walked toward him, her feet cutting open the circle.

And as she did, the magic gushed outward into the night.

11

MARIONETTE

A long, insidious scream bellowed along the air like the last war song sung by a dying solider. The old hag laughed, cackling between wheezing coughs.

"You did it, Fireheart!" the old woman said, gasping for air. She pointed a crooked finger.

Morganne and Bedivere followed her gaze toward the scream churning their blood thick and cold.

It was coming from Kay.

With ghastly movements and perverse jolts, Kay's body shuddered and jerked until he stood on his feet. Here, wobbling like a toddler standing for the first time, Kay's eyes snapped open. But they were not his intense blue eyes of charm and mischief, but rather red as the devil's own skin. And they stared into nothing and everything. Morganne sensed the vastness of the universe in those black, black pupils. His mouth opened, an unnatural movement like a marionette on performance.

"Fireheart," the voice said, and Morganne recognized the tone in a heartbeat. Not the deep, husky voice of Kay, but a time-worn tenor of ancient knowings. The voice she had felt in her mind.

Emrysa.

"You come, good. Your family are weakening under my blue flame. They have but hours before it will strip them of their memories and powers. You must come —"

"Am I not here?" Morganne bellowed, sickened as Kay's body lurched toward her like a living doll, arms outstretched, stare penetrating. "Tell me, tell me and I will come, *please.*"

Kay's—*Emrysa's*—right arm flung outward, gesturing to Angelfire, but that frightful stare remained fixed on Morganne. "Fetch me the horse. A spellbound witch like yourself cannot know such things. I need to share. I will share with the beast, and the beast will bring you to me."

Morganne shook her head, her trembling fingers steepled to her lips. "No," she whispered, not wanting her poor, innocent horse to suffer under Emrysa's demands—though she knew she must.

"Come!" screamed the voice from Kay's mouth; and Angelfire did.

He took slow and proud steps, like a warrior marching into a war he knew he couldn't win, but would battle for honor, regardless. His coat glistened shades of amber and lava as he passed the campfire with measured steps. He stood and tossed his head, his magnificent mane dancing like the firelight. Kay's body teetered over to the horse and placed a hand on the steed's forehead beneath his forelock. Angelfire took one step back, then steeled himself against his fear. His swishing tail the silent evidence of his discomfort.

Tears streamed down Morganne's face, warm and hot against the night. *My poor, brave horse.* She stepped forward, but Kay's head turned with an unnatural jolt, the red eyes boring into Morganne and stopping her from taking another step.

Bedivere hissed through his teeth. "I've got to do something." He strode forward. "Go, you wretched soul. I demand you to leave Kay's body. Leave him, *now!*"

Kay's head bent back, *too far back*, as though it may snap clean off. A chilling laugh erupted from his mouth.

Kay's arm flung from Angelfire's head toward Bedivere, sending the dark-haired knight flying backward through the nighttime air, his body crashing against a tree.

Bedivere landed in a heap.

"No!" screamed Morganne, running to the knight as he staggered to his feet.

A fox cried into the night. An owl hooted. Angelfire reared, screaming a neigh as chilling as a frost-laden grave. Morganne yelped, staring helplessly back at her horse. Kay's body turned, his face morphing now, aging and cursed. "The beast knows the way, and the beast will come. For he knows what will happen to his dear companions if he fails in his quest. I need not tell you what will happen if you fail in yours…"

Morganne turned, sprinting to Angelfire; his coat glistened, and his entire body trembled. She thudded against his body, embraced his hot, sweating coat as her own tears roared from within.

As her tears fell, the air in the forest softened, as if the world had been holding its breath, and now exhaled long and slow. Morganne looked around the dying campfire, the gypsy hag and carriage was gone, only a raven left in her place. Bedivere watched her with horror and something else behind those deep, dark eyes.

Then Kay dropped to the floor.

12

A DIFFERENT KIND OF MAGIC

"*N*o!" screamed Bedivere, dropping to his knees beside his friend's lifeless body.

"Is he breathing?" Morganne asked, heart racing as Bedivere bent his head close to Kay's gaunt face. She watched the boy's chest and saw no movement.

Bedivere jostled Kay into his arms, one arm under his neck, the other under his knees and stood. Kay's head fell backwards and Morganne gasped at the blueness of his lips, the grayness of his skin.

"He is barely breathing, I must get him to Camelot —the king's magician will know what to do."

Bedivere struggled with his friend's weight as he tried to hoist Kay into his saddle.

"Here, let me help." Morganne rushed to Bedivere's side, her entire body shaking with shock and guilt. This was all her fault. *Again.* Her hands trembled as she helped move Kay into place.

"It's okay, I can do this," Bedivere said, raising his voice when Morganne failed to step away from his task. "I said, I can do this!"

The venom in his words hit her like a slap to her face, and Morganne shot backward. Bedivere turned, his stare compelling her to step back further. Yet, as much as she hated the accusations laced in his beautiful dark eyes, she could not turn away. He was right; this was her fault. His face softened then, and he caught a tear that clung to Morganne's lower lashes with the pad of his thumb.

"I'm sorry, Morganne. Please forgive me. I'm just… I'm scared."

Morganne nodded. "Me too," she admitted.

"Come here," he whispered, pulling her into an embrace.

Morganne melted into his arms, her head resting on his chest. His heart pounded to the rhythm of her own. She wanted to stay for eternity in his safe arms but with reluctance, pulled away.

"The king's magician," Morganne whispered, staring up at Bedivere. "He knows of such magic, this…*dark magic?*" she cringed, holding her breath.

"Merlin? Dark magic? No, of course not. Arthur's

arse, you'll get yourself killed for treason for repeating such things," Bedivere said. He stared at her incredulous, his face a picture of both fear and concern. "Dark magic was, as you well know, outlawed centuries ago." He flung his arm toward Kay's motionless body slung over his horse's saddle. "For this very reason."

Morganne turned away from the truth of it and whispered so quietly that Bedivere had to step closer to hear.

"What did you say?" he asked, cursing his angry tone when he noticed Morganne's shoulders shuddering.

"I believe nothing else *but* dark magic can help him now."

Bedivere stamped the ground, sending dust swirling upward from the forest loam. He yelled with frustration, and punched into the nighttime air causing his horse to spook away from him, rocking Kay's body in the saddle.

"Damn it all!" Bedivere called, then calming himself when he saw the fear in the steed and his reflection in Morganne's emerald eyes. He took three measured breaths before nodding. "I hate to say this, but I think you are right," he said, softening his tone and holding her gaze.

To her surprise, Bedivere took both Morganne's

hands in his own, and she staggered at the heat of his palms.

He shook his head. "But I need to know how all this madness came to be. What did you do to awaken this evil being? You've been so secretive, but I'm involved now. You must tell me—why did you start this?"

Morganne wanted to pull away, to turn from him and hide her shame. She had a million reasons to justify her answers: jealousy, loneliness, betrayal, anger, but there was only one true reason. And it sounded as hollow and as pathetic in her mind as it did when it dripped from her tongue.

"I wanted to be magical," she said, the words choking and wavering as they left her quivering lips.

Bedivere caught a wisp of Morganne's auburn hair grazing her cheek. "You are the most magical being I have ever seen," he said, his dark eyes wide. "Magic…" he let go of her tresses, grazing her pale cheek with his dark fingers as he did so. "Magic, *real magic*," he tapped his heart three times with his fist, "lives here."

And despite everything, for one brief second, Morganne forgot herself, and felt her lips parting as Bedivere leant in close. The universe shrank to surround them in its embrace. The warmth of his breath touched her face.

A screech—and Angelfire plowed between them,

breaking the magic of the moment. He stamped a hoof, sending swirls of dust into the pre-dawn air, and tossed his head toward his back with impatience. Morganne did not need to hear Angelfire's words to understand his intention.

"We must go," Morganne said, breathless, holding Bedivere's hands in her own and her heart in her mouth.

A question hovered between them as Bedivere broke her gaze to look back at Kay's pitiful form and Camelot in the far distance.

"Together," said Bedivere. "We will find this witch together."

Morganne risked a smile and within moments, they were on their way.

And as silent as an assassin, the raven with the amber eye followed.

13

ANGELFIRE

*A*ngelfire pelted across the land, uncaring of the rough terrain.

Black and White. Shadowind and Moonglow, his companions and best friends both, were going to die.

He cared not about his bruised hooves; he had experienced worse. Nor did he care about his cramping muscles as his hind quarters powered and propelled his body forward. Angelfire did not care if he died trying to save them.

And try he did, scrambling over rocks, sliding down steep river banks, sloshing through ice-cold water that froze his tired legs and sucked the very air from his lungs. The Immortal One had shown him the way, and as they blurred through fields and valleys and mountain passes, Angelfire knew he was in no natural land.

Nature bent around him, opening old worlds and old paths neither walked nor galloped in centuries.

The faerie roads.

Treacherous lands of lies and trickery and deceit, yet he slowed not—cursing his inability to talk to the girl, Morganne. She needed his advice now more than ever, but as silent as a lightning-struck tree, he continued, heart clenching at the images of his fellow horses buckled under the weight of the blue flame. Dying, slowly and painfully whilst wrapped in cascading torrents of memories—sadness, fear, and terror. The flame was sucking the life from them, and though Angelfire tried not to think about it, the arduous journey was sucking the life out of *him*.

But on he galloped…

14

FALLEN

*H*ooves pounded the ground with relentless fury. Morganne had not spoken a word, neither Bedivere upon his giant white steed as they sliced through the air. He followed the little red horse, constantly grappling with Kay's corpse-like body that threatened to slip and fall, whilst battling to keep leading Kay's horse that lagged behind as they hurtled across the rough terrain.

Angelfire slowed to a shaky walk, his limbs weak beneath his sweating body.

"This place," Morganne said breathless, clutching her chest with one hand as she looked around. "This place is not natural."

They walked through a craggy pass; cavernous stones loomed over them like a threat. Leafless trees grew here and there through cracks and crevasses so deep they looked to have no end. On they continued, sloshing through a stream, the rocky riverbed and moss-covered stones making the horses slip and scramble. Morganne found it hard to breathe—the air dense as if stumbling into a room where the remnants of a heartbreaking argument lingered, its memory imprinted in the air, making it hard to swallow.

They rounded a bend, and the path opened to a wilderness more soul-sucking than breathtaking. An immense plateau spanned the horizon, desolate and empty bar scattered skeletal trees, whose naked branches reached upward like withered veins pleading for life from the sky. Towering over the vast wasteland rose a mountain peak with obscure turrets that jutted from its bulk, penetrating the sky bruised purple with dawn.

Morganne and Bedivere exchanged a silent glance, hesitating to say the words. But they knew they had reached the place. A blackness called to them like a morbid curiosity—a pulling at lung and liver despite the heart's protest.

They rode toward the mountain, dwarfed by the surrounds as its shadow loomed across the land and engulfed them in a shroud of darkness.

Morganne pointed a trembling finger. "Do you see

that?"

Bedivere nodded, jaw clenched.

At the base of the mountain, a dark cavernous hole opened, and beside it, a stone carved as a rearing horse rose from the ground, its limbs too lifelike to be the work of a craftsman. Wordlessly, they continued until they reached the carving at the entrance of the cave. Each step closer whispering a promise of sorrow and dread that somehow etched itself on the face of the stone horse.

Angelfire shuddered and groaned beneath Morganne, then dropped in a heap to the floor.

Morganne slammed into the ground beside her horse and scrambled toward him with grazed knees. "Angelfire?" she sobbed, placing a hand on his neck slick with sweat.

Angelfire groaned. He tried to lift his head but failed, its heavy weight crashing to the floor once more. "Angel?" she said again, this time the name choking in her throat like a last goodbye. He rolled his dark orbs toward her, exposing the whites of his eyes. His nostrils flared, quivering as he gasped for air.

"He has exhausted himself," Bedivere said, dismounting quickly. He placed a hand on Morganne's shoulder; it shook beneath his touch.

She shot to her feet. "I'll go. I'll face Emrysa and

force her to make him better, and I won't give her what she wants until she does."

Morganne turned to run, but Bedivere refused to let go of her hands.

"And what is it she wants?" Bedivere asked.

Morganne turned away, and Bedivere looked back at his lifeless friend still slung over his horse. "You shall not go alone. I will accompany you."

"You cannot. Please, Bedivere, you must stay here, you must stay with Angelfire and Kay to protect them, and…" Morganne paused, pulling her hands from Bedivere's and flinging her arms toward the cave like an incantation. "If anything happens to me in there, at least you'll survive to find someone, *anyone*, who can help."

Her eyes shot to Angelfire as he groaned on the ground, his body heat swirling as mist around him in the cold dawn air. It was the desperate look on her face that caused Bedivere's shoulders to drop. Defeated.

He nodded once, tapping his heart three times with his fist. Morganne tried to smile, repeating the silent gesture worth a million words. And she turned, disappearing into the cursed chamber that reeked of broken promises and deceit.

15

UNDOING

*H*er footsteps echoed as she stepped into the darkness—the light from the entrance behind her casting an eerie blue glow upon the wet walls. Drops of water fell in the distance, a deep and tinny sound hinting at the depths of the hovel. Rats scuttled past Morganne's feet, but she pressed deeper into the chamber, Angelfire's pain-riddled moans and Kay's lifeless body still filling her mind.

Deeper. A voice whispered, overcoming Morganne's thoughts. *Deeper still.*

The urge to follow the voice continued, pulling at sinew and bone, and despite the stench of death and decay, Morganne crept forward until the light behind her disappeared. The darkness was not the type to allow her eyes to adjust to its gloom as they would when waking in the stillness of night. Despite blinking several times in the hope to renew her sight to the blackness surrounding her, the darkness did not clear. Instead, Morganne cast one hand ahead, while the fingers of her other trailed the damp, sticky wall as she edged deeper.

With each step the air cooled, wrapping itself around her like a coffin, and Morganne felt something other than her hands guided her.

A scratch, like a match striking stone stopped her. Ahead, a small glow emanated. A small *blue* glow.

The blue flame.

"Show yourself!" Morganne called into the darkness.

Her voice bounced back from all directions, twenty times or more, each one sharing the horror in her tone. A whisper of wind lifted her hair, and a swoop of feathers gathered close; the light touch of a raven's wing brushed her cheek. It cawed into the echoing blackness and a wild, wicked laugh cackled into the fetid air.

A strike of lightning erupted when raven and the Immortal One met; the blue glow exploded, lighting the entire cavern. Morganne gasped at the depthless chasm surrounding her. She staggered backward, but the heel of her right foot found no purchase and she teetered on the brink before righting herself. Morganne swayed upon the pillar, whose surrounding depths stretched into the core of the universe itself. Bile rose to her throat as she realized she had made the entire journey this way—from pillar to pillar, like morbid stepping stones, yet instead of a river flowing around them, there was nothing but bottomless darkness.

"How?" she questioned herself, wishing she had something to grasp to stop vertigo swaying her vision.

"Walk," ordered the now-familiar voice.

Emrysa was far enough away that Morganne could only make out her hunched form and blackened cloak hanging over bony shoulders. A hood rose over the crone's head, hiding her face in shadows and darkness.

"Walk!" This time Emrysa's voice boomed from walls slick with brown moss shining under the unnatural glow in her hands.

Morganne placed a foot forward and hesitated as it hovered over the chasm. She shook her head, trembling. "I... *I can't!*" and though she hated herself for it, Morganne sobbed.

"No harm will come to you if you do as I say," the witch promised. She pointed toward Morganne, then crawled her fingers back into her palm commanding Morganne forward. "No harm will come to your *family*, if you do as I say."

Sounds erupted around the cave that Morganne both recognized and despised. Her sisters' screams formed, bouncing from the walls in wails of fear, growing in volume and intensity. The sound of tinny water dripping morphed into her mother's tears. Somehow, from the ground beneath her feet, a trembling groan erupted and Morganne knew it to be the pain from Angelfire. And a choking call spluttered in her mind; it sounded like Kay.

Morganne braced herself, not knowing if these were mere illusions, threats, or something far worse. She had no choice but to make her way across the impossible path. Squeezing her eyes shut, Morganne took her first step, stones cracking and forming under her feet as she did so. She released a measured breath though her jaw still clenched with fear and anger both.

"Yes, yes. Come, Fireheart." The witch cackled once again.

Morganne fought a paralyzing urge and sprinted across, the ground reforming beneath her feet. Breathless, she reached Emrysa, and the witch looked upward, pulling her hood back to get a better look at the girl.

"You do me a great service by seeking me," Emrysa said, and smiled like a cat before pouncing on an unsuspecting mouse. She flickered in and out of view, like a mirage or an illusion, or a memory of what the witch once was.

"I had no choice," Morganne said, recoiling at the sight and stench of the centuries-old hag up close. Her withered skin looked paper thin, but despite the flickering transparency of her fragile form, the witch's life force was astounding. Morganne tried to hold Emrysa's stare, but the witch's eyes, entirely black, caused Morganne to turn away with repulsion.

"You," Emrysa said, reaching for Morganne's hand. "You have no idea how your call woke me from my slumber. I was merely a thought, a cursed memory, before you breathed life back into me."

"I did not mean to," Morganne spat, returning her gaze with her chin held high, feigning confidence. The old woman laughed and the raven on her shoulder flapped its wings. Morganne mustered her courage to continue. "You need something from me, I understand that now. And I, in return, need something from you."

"You dare to barter?" A lopsided grin split the hag's withered face in two. For a few seconds, the witch's form was almost perfectly physical and Morganne noticed her peeling skin.

Morganne took three measured breaths, trying to remember who she was. Eldest sister, voice of reason. "Yes, I dare to barter. I know you cannot leave this hole, or you would already have fled this woebegone place centuries ago. You are held here."

Emrysa nodded, and flakes of skin fell from her face as she did. "You may not wield magic, but you have sense young Fireheart, and *passion*. I long for that passion in my own veins."

Morganne gulped. "If you undo the wrongs I've brought on by summoning your memory back into this world, then perhaps you'll feel that passion once again."

Emrysa turned to her raven and stroked its head. When she turned back to Morganne, her face was a mask of concern and her voice as sweet as overripe berries. "And what wrongs might these be?"

"You know very well!" Morganne spat. The ground trembled, pieces of rock disappearing into the chasm below.

"Tread carefully," the old witch warned, shaking her hooked finger in warning.

Morganne fought the instinct to back away and held her ground, though beads of sweat formed at her temples despite the cold and damp of the enormous cave.

"My family, the boy outside, *my horse,*" she pleaded. "They are all innocents in this stupid game, they should not have to pay with their lives. *I* brought your memory back into this world, *I* should be the one to pay the price. Please, whatever it takes, release them from your hold."

The old woman smiled and nodded, thoughtful. This concerned Morganne. After centuries of imprisonment, the witch was in no rush to exit the place, she had patience, which meant she was dangerous. Morganne's heart beat triple time.

"I will need three things for the three undoings," the witch said. She paused, then licked her lips, her tongue pale and white. "And one more to answer your prayer to me."

"What prayer?" Morganne shot back.

"Magic, dear girl. Did I not promise to make you more powerful than all?"

"Yes," Morganne said, her brow as creased as the craggy rocks around her. "But I care not for the stupid magic any longer. I just want everything to go back to normal. I just want my family safe. Forget about that stupid oath—"

"But I cannot!" screamed the witch. She lurched, bracing both hands to Morganne; a blue light charged from her fingertips, crackling through the air toward the redheaded girl. "You are oath-bound, not just to me but to the nature of things. Nothing without consequence. No action without reaction. You *will give* me the three things for the undoing spells, and you *will give* me one more for the oath. Then, only then, can we untie our bonds."

She flicked her fingers and lightning grabbed Morganne in its clutches. Morganne fell to her knees with the pain of the blue light surging through her veins—though she needed no pain to force her into a decision. The decision had already been made.

"I'll do it," she swore, the light binding her still. "I'll do whatever it takes to save my family. Even if that means I release you from this hellhole."

Emrysa erupted with crazed laugher, and the world seemed to turn away.

16

BLOOD OATHS

*T*he light splintered into a billion pieces, dancing like falling snow under a blue moon glow, and Morganne had the chilling feeling that the world as she knew it, was already dead.

"Your blood for your family, your heart for the boy, your strength for the fire horse, and… something else to break the bond." Emrysa could not hide the look of glee and greed in her eyes. "Your life."

Those black orbs pulsed and danced in the blue light, and Morganne could see the fear in her own reflection staring back.

"You will take my life…" Morganne's innards lurched, as if a hole deeper than the crevices below her entered her soul. "You will kill me?"

"Oh, I won't kill you, of that I promise. Now, follow me," Emrysa said.

The witch turned and shuffled deeper into the cave, her physical form flickering like a candle flame in the wind. Feet sloshed in rank and stale water that smelt of broken promises and guilty secrets. Morganne followed, each step her own undoing, but shuffled on regardless. The witch led her to what once would have been a grand fountain, now sitting decrepit in the center of an oval opening. Morganne had to tilt her head back to see the structure in its entirety. Bones as white as ghosts interlinked to form the basin, and the rim around the structure stood on a base of skulls. Morganne clutched her chest as she peered in, but the fountain had long ago run dry, the bones cracked with the passing of time.

"Your arm," Emrysa demanded, holding her hand out expectantly. Morganne responded, shivering at the witch's touch as her wrist was grabbed with more force than the old hag's fragile-looking hands seemed able. With her free hand, Emrysa stroked the soft and sensitive skin on the underside of Morganne's forearm, relishing in the beauty of its youth. She snarled then, and pressed into Morganne's skin with a nail as sharp as a raven's claw. She cawed with fiendish pride as a prick of red swelled around her nail, and Morganne gasped, gritting her teeth with feigned bravery. Though her bowels felt weak, she clenched her fear inside.

Emrysa pulled Morganne closer to the fountain, turning her arm and skewering the nail deeper so blood trickled into the basin. Morganne gasped again, pulling back.

"Stand still," the witch demanded, yanking Morganne's arm toward herself.

Her blood dripped on the top of the skulls forming the basin. Black smoke swirled from the crimson liquid that looked like dark ink in the hollow blue light. The witch finally flung Morganne's arm back at her, and stared at the bowl. Morganne compressed the wound to stop the bleeding though it still crept through the gap of her fingers as she watched her own blood in the basin swell like a mini ocean—crashing with dreadful red waves as it spread outwards and upwards. Soon, the entire fountain roared with cascading blood, filling the cavern with a sweet and sickly metallic twang.

She recoiled when the witch submerged those withered hands, her arms, her *face* in the fountain, drinking in the taste of Morganne.

"Oh dear goddess," Morganne said, gagging.

Emrysa turned, bloodied face and hair, and somehow more solid than she had appeared moments before. "Your family is safe now. The blood oath complete."

"How can I tell if you are lying?" Morganne demanded, finding a strength in the little hope she held.

The witch shrugged and smiled again, her rotten teeth dripping with red like a feasting wolf. Morganne turned away, but not before noticing the witch's skin blossoming, pale and smooth.

"And now, your heart for the boy."

For a moment, Morganne hesitated. She did not *owe* Kay her heart, she did not even know him. Why should she give *him* her heart? If anyone was to have it, her heart was for Bedivere. Brave, beautiful Bedivere. The witch cackled as if reading her thoughts.

"Your knight will forever blame you for my little puppet's death if you forfeit his life. He will forever know you to be a selfish, greedy, little girl," the witch barked. "And Kay is not only his best friend, but his cousin bound in blood and love."

Morganne chastised herself. *How could I consider such a thing as to leave Kay to die because of my own heartless fear?* "Why would you want my heart?" Morganne said. "It is nothing if not weak and pathetic."

"It's not your pity I need, girl. Now, come."

The witch held out her arms as if welcoming a

loved one into an embrace. Clenching her fists, Morganne took two nervous steps toward the witch's open arms, and Emrysa held her, pulling her so close, Morganne had to hold her breath against the stench of death.

Morganne's heart pounded, louder and louder, ricocheting against her ribs. The sound boomed from both outside and inside, bouncing against the walls of the cave and throbbing in her head.

Da-dum.

Da-dum.

Da-dum.

Faster and faster, it strained against a violent grasp.

A searing pain, and Morganne screeched into the darkness; a ripping sensation pulling at her very soul. Her heartbeat quickened until it was no longer the double-sounding beat she had felt her entire life, but a sorrowful, singular sound.

The pain ebbed. Sound diminished. And somehow Morganne knew only half her heart pounded in her chest—its beat reduced to a mournful dirge, echoing sadness in a chamber that had once been full. She sobbed, clenching her broken heart and fell to the floor with a splash. And on the cold, wet ground, Morganne wept.

But while half a heart brought Morganne to her

knees, Emrysa clutched her chest in wonderment. Her body glowed, losing its deathly pallor and transparency; age spots disappeared, and her hair—the knotted, colorless, tangled mess, grew into red tresses, thick and lush and full.

Emrysa placed her hand on Morganne's head as the girl cried on the floor. "What strength you have left is almost too easy to take. This, for the fire horse."

Morganne's life-force diminished further, and it was not just strength that fled from her body like a herd of spooked horses, but hope and belief and anything strong and true.

She wailed, clutching her broken body and soul, holding herself in a tight embrace to salvage anything left of herself from seeping from her bones. "I have nothing left to give you," she cried, knowing the witch had one more desire before she broke the oath tie.

"But you are wrong, Fireheart," Emrysa said. Her voice was no longer raspy and cruel. It was silken. *Familiar.*

Morganne looked upward and her words caught in her throat. Emrysa was no longer a hag, an ancient witch of decay and bones. She was radiant. She was young. She was the image of Morganne herself. Morganne tried to scramble to her feet but fell back to her knees.

"What? What are doing? How can this be?" She spat the words like broken arrows from a flimsy bow.

Emrysa laughed. "The one thing I needed for the oath bond, was...*your life.*"

"You said you wouldn't kill me, you promised!" Morganne screamed, pulling at her hair, rocking on the spot. The woman before her smiled, a chilling smile that would never belong to Morganne though the face was just the same.

"Oh, darling girl," Emrysa said, like a gentle mother concerned for her child's pain. "I will not *kill* you. I'm doing something far, far worse."

The witch snapped her thumbs and fingers, and the ground around Morganne shuddered and crumbled, thundering into the chasm below. A canyon separated her from Emrysa—separated her from escape, from life, from *everyone and everything.* A deep, dark nothingness as deep as Morganne's regret.

"But fear not," Emrysa said as she strode away, her old black cloak morphing into flaming red silks that trailed the floor behind her as she walked. She hesitated, her fingers reaching for the mark she already knew to be in place at her collarbone.

The mark of the dark. Two crescent moons back to back, like hooks, clawing the witch into its darkness. "This is not a complete transformation, not yet—even *I* do not possess the power for such things. But if the boy should love me, if he should see me as you and love me in your place, then the transformation will be complete and we will both have what we want."

The ground tumbled and disappeared as she left.

"Both have what we want?" Morganne screamed and sobbed over crashing rocks. "How is any of this what *I* want?"

Emrysa stopped and turned, her emerald eyes as fiery as flames. "Because if I transform, *you*, dear girl, shall forever transform too… into the bones and skin I leave behind. *You* will become Emrysa." She paused, cocking her head to the side. "Fireheart, why do you look so sad? You should smile, did you not once wish to be the most powerful witch? Well, you shall. While our transformation takes place, you shall have all my magic, but alas, you will also bear the curse your family placed on me all those centuries ago. Forever." She shook her head. "All that power, and nowhere to go."

And Emrysa departed the cavern leaving Morganne alone on her small island of stone and tears.

17

A WITCH'S STEED

*E*mrysa strode toward her freedom, leaving behind the clutches of the living hell that had imprisoned her for centuries. Young, fresh blood pumped around her body, and the witch reveled in her fine limbs, soft skin, the mass of red curls tumbling down her back. Her eyes, so accustomed to utter blackness, squinted when a touch of dim light splintered upon wet rocks by the faraway exit. She prowled, taking steady, measured steps despite a rapid heartbeat, taking her time to welcome the light back into her new, borrowed body. To welcome life *itself.*

But even Emrysa, for the hundreds of years she dreamt of walking back into the world, hesitated as she reached the threshold. To realize one of her most sought-after desires was not the ecstasy she imagined, and instead, a paralysis of fear and doubt and disbelief heaved in the pit of her stomach. Her emerald eyes welled with tears that had long ago dried and she stood, silent, trying to gain her composure…

She stepped out into the weak morning sun.

The first thing she noticed was birdsong, the chirps and warbles of finches and sparrows that flitted over the borders of the faerie realms with ignorant bliss. Then, the air. Emrysa closed her eyes and breathed the sweet taste of freedom with ravenous gulps—she almost laughed with joy when the fresh air filled her rank-stained lungs. She swirled with pure pleasure—the soft morning wind a playful dance through her tousled red locks and gown.

A gasp soiled her bliss. Her eyes flung open, and there he was.

Bedivere, his scarlet and gold cape shining in the gloom of the vast, rocky plateau. His black eyes shining all the more.

She should have been prepared. Emrysa was not a young harlot nor a whimsical maiden with her head in books filled with romance and petty affairs of the heart. Emrysa was the Immortal One, older than time itself and crueler than winter's frost. She had seen the boy through her visions, thanks to the pitiful child she left wallowing in despair.

But still… those eyes.

Emrysa stood like a work of art, relishing the admiration and inspection of the boy as he stared in awe. She followed his eyes, looking down at herself in her flaming red silk. Yes, crimson, it was a good choice. Her lips parted into a smile.

"You—you—" he steeled himself, clearing his throat. For composure's sake, he turned away, shaking his thoughts from his mind, though not his face. When he spoke again, his voice was sturdy and deep, but his eyes still stared with awe. "Are you okay? What happened in there? The witch?"

She smiled and cast his questions aside with an elegant flick of her hand.

"One question at a time, dear boy. We need not worry about her," Emrysa said, enjoying her effect on him. Yet a dagger of a thought pierced her mind. It was not *she* he saw, but the girl. Black crept around Emrysa's heart, its rapid beat slowed, the magic lost. Bedivere's face morphed from mesmerized to agonized. He turned to Kay, who lay on the rocky ground, a saddle bag under his head as a pillow, and his cape wrapped around him like a blanket—his face whiter than death. Beside Emrysa's puppet-boy, the red horse groaned with short, sharp breaths.

"They've got worse, both of them," Bedivere said,

his face painted with the agony that comes with waiting for another to decide the fate of a life. "Did you barter? Did you convince the witch to help?"

Emrysa frowned; she wanted Bedivere to run to her, to embrace her and set the true transformation in place right away, but the darkened mark still itched on her skin like a threat. Emrysa pulled the collar of her dress closer to her neck and hissed under her breath before resigning herself to play her part.

"The witch, she gave me something—something special, look," Emrysa cooed, trying to imitate Morganne's soft tones. She placed her hands on Angelfire's cold yet sweaty body as he rasped with labored breaths. From her hands, blue tendrils of smoke wrapped around the horse's body, cocooning him in a mist of other worldliness. Bedivere stepped back, cautious, thinking of the eerie glow that accompanied Kay while the witch spoke through him. But the soft blue light healed this time, pulsating stronger as the horse's breath relaxed, his coat dried and began to shine. In moments, Angelfire rose to his hooves and shook his body. He stepped forward but before Emrysa could soothe him, Angelfire reared.

You! he said in her mind, knowing the witch at once. He reared again, boxing his forelegs outward to strike her to the ground. He shrieked a neigh in an attempt to alert the knight of the deception.

Oh shut up you insolent nag, Emrysa spat back into his mind. She flicked her fingers at him, and with it a coldness seeped through his veins, shuddering as it reached his heart and mind. He no longer formed the thoughts he knew he had—they flitted from his mind like forgotten dreams at daybreak and were locked inside him like a silent scream. Angelfire tossed his head against the words he could not stop from penetrating his mind.

I command the horse to say no more
Binding him unto my law
To do exactly as I need
And do the work of a witch's steed.

"All better," she said aloud, patting Angelfire, and he accepted—only a tiny part of his mind recoiled, his body and soul bound to the spell. A spiteful smile crept across Emrysa's face and she turned, then staggered. With a gasp, the witch stared at her hands—magic drained from them, ebbing away. *Of course.* Emrysa was using Morganne's physical form as a vessel—meaning she did not have the ability, *nor permission,* from nature to replenish her own magic after she used it until the full transformation was complete.

"Pathetic," Emrysa muttered, her features fuming

at the dwindling magic and the burden of wearing a mortal's body.

Bedivere narrowed his eyes.

She turned, plastering a beatific smile across her face and without realizing, licked her lips at his stare. He raised a quizzical eyebrow.

"And Kay?" he asked. "You can help him, can you not?" Bedivere rubbed his temples, then pinched the bridge of his nose, his voice rising in panic. "Can you not help him?"

Emrysa cast a downward glance at the pale knight on the ground before her. *An oath is an oath.* The pathetic, spellbound girl had given half her heart in payment for Kay's health—though Morganne was yet to learn what that would mean... not that she could ever leave the clutches of the hovel.

"No," she said.

Bedivere smiled at first, a smile that arrives with the sudden impact of disbelief and denial. He shook his head, the color fading from his cinnamon cheeks. "What—but...?" he gulped, and his dark eyes watered as the truth sank into his bones.

"What I mean is," Emrysa said, calculating her plan. "I can't help him *here.* We must get back to my homestead."

He paced away from her, covering his open mouth

with his hand. Bedivere shot her a stare, looked back at Kay, and then toward the distant hills in which awaited Camelot.

Emrysa turned her back to hide her lips parting in a snarl. "The witch explained that my family hold the answers," Emrysa lied with urgent tones. She turned and stood before Bedivere as he paced. Emrysa grabbed his sweating hands in her own, hoping to tear his eyes away from her puppet on the ground. "He *will* get well at home, Bedivere, of this I know. She promised."

Emrysa nodded and Bedivere found himself nodding along with her.

"Okay, okay," he said, taking two slow, measured breaths. "So we ride back to your homestead—are you sure we shouldn't take him back to Camelot, back to Merlin?"

"*Merlin?*" Emrysa raged. She dropped Bedivere's hands and clenched her own into tight fists. Her nostrils flared. "What would *he* understand of such magic? He's a fourth-rate magician if ever I've known one."

Bedivere cocked his head to the side, like a dog trying to comprehend nonsensical words. He watched the witch through narrow eyes. "I thought you knew not of Merlin until I spoke of him—in fact, he's a closely guarded secret, Morganne. What could you possibly know of his magic and abilities?"

He stepped away from her, eyeing her crimson silks from head to toe, yet this time Emrysa did not feel admired but scrutinized. Mortals were so complicated. So riddled with ridiculous emotions…*emotions I crave to hold once more*, she thought in the deepest part of her half-heart. She sighed, closing her eyes to the boy with the fierce stare, and tried to recount the human emotions she once felt so long ago. She had to make him love her.

Somewhere, in the farthest reaches of her mind, she caught a whisper of compassion—the delicate emotion to feel *for* someone else. She allowed that clinging remnant of emotion to wrap around her thoughts, her body, and her words, so when she next spoke, it was a gentle whisper belonging to Morganne.

"I'm sorry, I should not have said that. It's just something the witch told me. I'm scared, Bedivere— I'm scared for Kay. I'm scared… for *us*." Bedivere softened then and took her hands once more. Emrysa looked up at him through Morganne's emerald eyes. "For all the witch promised, how can we trust her?"

"I don't know…" Bedivere said. "Perhaps we'll know in here."

He tapped his heart three times with his fist and Emrysa smiled.

"Come," she said. "Let's make haste to my homestead."

He kissed her forehead, and a tsunami of new emotions—and new life—flooded into her.

It was happening…

18

A STRONGER HEARTBEAT

*E*mrysa flashed a smile at Bedivere as they rode side-by-side, hoping to get a reaction. She did not, and Emrysa recoiled at her pettiness. Yes, it was important to get the boy to fall in love with her so she could keep the vessel of Morganne's body, but the longer they rode, the more bitter her thoughts became. And she would not allow mortal, dizzy desires to shade her real cause.

Now she smiled for herself, a secret smile full of irony as they rode toward the Cheval homestead and overdue revenge. It was, after all, the Cheval family whose bloodline incarcerated her into the depths of dread and forgotten memories. Knowing it was a Cheval that brought her back from a fate worse than death gave a certain poetic justice to her betrayal all those centuries ago. Knowing she would kill the family in Morganne's skin was a masterpiece in retribution.

But still, for all these thoughts, the boy's sullen moods were beginning to grind against her bones.

Days had passed and Bedivere's moods altered from urgent, to angry, to morose, and now, finally, silence. And Emrysa could not stand it. Yes, of course she had the ability to pull on the power of nature and use her remaining magic to whisk them back to Morganne's homestead in an instant—it would cost her a lot of magic in the process, but it was certainly within her power, even within the mortal frame hanging around the essence of her soul.

But she needed reserves for the Cheval onslaught of which she played over and over in her mind. And she needed time to allow the boy to continue falling in love with her, and if not *her*, then the *idea* of her if she was to revel in her stolen youth once more. But several days later, Bedivere still made no attempt to kiss her, and instead, side-eyed her when he thought she wouldn't notice, and watched her with cool curiosity when she did.

"We will be there by dawn," Emrysa said, and suppressed the urge to send a soothing spell to the boy.

She could not have a hand in changing his moods with the use of magic *and* seal nature's deal.

The low sun cast shards of gold across the emerald forest and Emrysa sighed. "I am tired," she added, feigning a suppressed yawn, hoping to get close to the boy around the campfire.

"As you wish," Bedivere said, matter of fact.

Emrysa's fingers clenched around Angelfire's reins, and he came to an abrupt halt, throwing his head in the air when the bit pulled against his gums. "Oh, stand still," she commanded, and the little red horse obliged. The witch narrowed her eyes and watched as Bedivere pulled his steed to a halt, dismounted, and began setting up camp.

He doubts me, she feared, and then aloud, "It seems the closer we get to my homestead, the more sullen you become."

He looked at her, incredulous. "And what do you expect?" he spat.

Emrysa swallowed her frustration, watching as he removed Kay from his steed with the gentleness of a father carrying a child. He placed the sleeping knight on a blanket of furs, his jaw clenched.

That marionette is more trouble than he's worth. Emrysa wondered how she could deal with Kay without disrupting her plan to get her body, revenge, *and*, she thought with a surprising amount of desire, *the boy*.

She dismounted, giving Angelfire an antagonizing pat, knowing he could do nothing but accept it as she tethered him. She knelt beside Kay, placing her hand on his forehead and risked a little magic to seep from her fingers.

Breathe more life into his skin
Let his wake from slumber begin
Take it slow to you I pray
And only wake when I say.

As she thought the words Kay's pale complexion blossomed, the apples of his cheeks turning pink, his lips reddening. His eyes flickered behind his closed lids.

"Did you see that?" Bedivere said. He smiled like a child at Emrysa then squeezed Kay's shoulder. "Kay, can you hear me?"

Kay's eyes flicked once more, opening for a breath, and closed again, a gentle snore escaping him.

"He's waking," Bedivere said, but instead of jubilance, he collapsed to the ground, rubbing his temples and taking deep breaths. "I thought I had lost him," he muttered.

Emrysa softened, taking hold of Bedivere's arm. "He looks so healthy now, perhaps he will wake before dawn."

Bedivere's face crumpled, his dark eyes rimmed with red and tears. Emrysa took the opportunity, and his face, in her hands. "He will be fine. I know it, and —" she looked down, feigning bashfulness, allowing the blood to rise at her cheeks before looking back at the boy through her eyelashes. "—I'm sure, *we* will be fine, too."

Bedivere smiled then, the relief in his face softening his features and Emrysa smiled back at him, truly smiling, from the half-heart thudding in her chest. Bedivere thumped his own chest three times, then reached for her hand, pulling her closer.

Emrysa's breath pulled short, spellbound by the look in the knight's eyes as he stared at her. His fingers traced her jaw line, her lips, and she felt herself shudder, forgetting the centuries of darkness, forgetting the living nightmare of cursed bindings and unfair accusations. Her lips trembled now as he moved close, his warm breath on her skin, his hand lost in the cascade of her red curls tumbling down her back.

"Kiss me," he whispered, his face inches from her own. His eyes stared into her soul.

Emrysa prayed to a God she did not believe in, reveling in the purity of love and lust and mortal desire. And like a secret promise, their lips touched, and Emrysa melted, whisked away by another form of magic altogether. In the midst of blissful pleasure, Emrysa felt a change from within. Her heart beat a little louder now, a little stronger. And she smiled because she knew Morganne's heart was weakening in the process and the transformation was taking place. And within a rushing heartbeat, she forgot all about the girl and revenge, and lost herself entirely to the kiss.

19

PUTRID PUDDLES

Morganne stared at her hands.

"No, *no!*" she cried with the pitiful amount of strength she had left in her body.

Her skin grew old like a page from a forgotten book, and she could not help but think of the grimoire she wished she had never found. Her nails crumbled and cracked, yellowing as they grew and stretched into talons. Age spots leaked from her fingers up her forearms. She trembled, feeling the ancient world within her brittling bones.

"What's happening to me?" Morganne cried, but she knew.

Which was why she feared for her heart the most— and not only because it weakened, its dull single beat quieting still. She felt the pain in the knowing, the knowing that Bedivere had failed to recognize the deceit—fooled by the witch Emrysa with her red locks and redder silken dress. Which only meant one thing; he was never truly in love with her, but only with her appearance. She felt sickened and hopeless and doomed. While somewhere out there, near home and loved ones, the knight continued to kiss the witch. Morganne's world collapsed as she dropped to her knees in the darkness, heaving deep and heavy sobs into the putrid puddles surrounding her.

20

QUESTIONS

*E*mrysa cast her eyes to the knight sleeping bedside her as the campfire crackled. She rose with stealth, holding her breath and keeping her eyes pinned on Bedivere to ensure she did not wake him. The flames gave her enough light to see, yet hid her in shadows as she tiptoed around the fire to Kay. She knelt and spat a silent curse into the night for the magic she would lose for this wasteful spell, and placed a hand on Kay's forehead, Emrysa spoke to the nature of things within her mind once more.

Wake the boy but not his thoughts
As he gallops home to Camelot Court
All my secrets — force him to keep
While his memories will be out of reach
He'll seem himself in his own land

But his body I shall command
To do exactly as I say
So wake him now, without delay.

Kay rubbed his eyes, then stretched his arms above his head, producing a huge wide-mouthed yawn and sigh. Emrysa put her fingers to her lips to quiet him, and he obliged. Rising stiffly, he ran a hand through his blond hair that stuck up in all directions and looked around himself, confused and dazed. He opened his lips to speak, but Emrysa shook her head.

Leave. You will write a note to your dear friend telling him you have returned to Camelot to convalesce, and that he should continue on his quest. Say not a word, and you leave, now, with haste.

He raised his eyebrows, shrugged, and rummaged through Bedivere's saddlebags stacked on the forest floor beside him. With a smile that split his sharp face, he produced a small set of scrolls, a tiny inkwell and a quill, whose feathers sat as askew as his messy hair. Emrysa stifled a laugh, his mannerisms reminding her of a compliant puppy.

Leaning against a tree, Kay paused, staring at the quill and scroll in turn, then wrote, his writing scraggly with the bark beneath the paper. He folded it, placed it next to Bedivere with a self-congratulating smirk, and saddled his horse in silence.

Emrysa watched on, nodding in cool approval until he turned and rode away into the shadows. Then, she returned to her own knight with the smugness of a woman who has a man's undivided attention. Nothing could distract dearest Bedivere now. Nothing could stop the transformation taking place. She curled up next to the boy, and, content with the knowledge she would finally get everything she always wanted, Emrysa fell fast asleep.

SEVERAL HOURS LATER, Bedivere awoke and watched the beautiful redhead sleep beside the fireside; the flickering flames danced from her pale skin in patterns. She breathed softly, and almost looked to smile in her sleep. Yet this sight did not make Bedivere's heart burst as it should.

Something's different. He cocked his head in study, as if seeing her from a different angle could stir his stagnant emotions. He had kissed her, and yet for all the promise their *almost kiss* had brought before she went into the witch's cave, this kiss was just... wet and empty. There was no passion, no *need,* and though he did not wish to acknowledge it, certainly no love.

Which was queer indeed.

Because Bedivere was head over heels in love with Morganne.

Eyes wide, he stared into the fire that seemed to burn a warning in his heart and soul. Behind him, Angelfire snorted, and another curiosity crossed his mind. The softness with which Morganne usually rode, as if she were not commanding the horse at all, had been different riding back from the cave. Angelfire had been subdued, he had blamed this on the horse's need to recover from his exhaustion. But there was something else too. Bedivere rose, striding toward the horse tethered to a tree.

Tethered.

Morganne had never before tied her horse, trusting him to graze and stay close by, not like his own steed who would bolt back to the comfort of his warm Camelot stable and a bucket of warm oats with only half a chance. He smoothed Angelfire's broad forehead, looking over toward his own horse in the darkness.

"Wait…" His hand dropped from Angelfire's head. He shook his head. *Bloody horses. Where has Kay's steed got to?*

He checked the area for signs of the horse's escape, he wouldn't go far from his companions. Still, he'd rather not go chasing horses in the pitch darkness of midnight. *Strange.* He didn't see a broken rope from the horse pulling back. In fact, he saw nothing at all. He turned to the shadows where Kay lay, next to the saddlery and packs. His brow creased, and he walked closer to better see.

"He's gone?"

"Bedivere," a voice as sweet as sugar called him and somehow, it made his teeth itch. "Come back to the fireside with me, keep me warm."

"Morganne, get up," he pressed, scuttling to her side. "It's Kay, he's *gone!*"

That's when his eyes fell upon the scroll nestled against fallen leaves and the forest loam. He grabbed it, nearly tearing the paper with the force in which he opened it. His eyes scanned the words, and the paper fluttered to the ground.

"He says he has gone back to Camelot." Bedivere stared into the flames.

The witch sat up, smiling. "Is that not good news? This means we can make haste to my homestead to check my family without worrying about Kay's health. If he managed to write and saddle his horse whilst we slept, he must be better. Come on, come here next to me and let us rest. Tomorrow will be a big day."

Bedivere watched her for a few thoughtful moments —the thick, lush red curls cascading down her shoulders to the curve of her waist. Her red silk dress clinging to her skin, the furs he had offered her to lie on soft and warm.

He nodded. "Yes," he said, and wandered back to her side, nestling into thick furs and curls.

"That's better," she said, leaning into his chest. Within moments, her soft purring snores confirmed she was asleep.

Bedivere closed his eyes, but for him, sleep did not come. He lay there, feeling like a fly caught in a spider's web as questions formed and reformed in his mind. And the biggest one of all, was the lie on the note. Kay could not have written it. Because Kay, for all his intelligence and valor, could not read or write.

He only hoped this inner truth had not surfaced too late…

INNER TRUTH

*M*organne gasped, a sudden strength swelling within her weak pulse. She sat up, dizzy in the darkness. She held her withered and aged hands close to her face and watched the decay flaking her skin up to her elbows. But as Morganne stared at her arms in the gloom, she noticed that slowly, as slowly as the unseen moon moves throughout the day, the rot was beginning to recede. She took a breath as the softness of her skin returned—feeling it rather than seeing it in the utter blackness—and she sighed with the sleekness of her blood as it flowed in her veins, the lightness of her bones deep within.

"He knows," Morganne said, daring to hope. "He knows it is the witch Emrysa, not me."

Inside the secret chamber of her half-beating heart, Morganne pleaded for this hope to be true. Then his words came back to her, somehow bounding from the walls from the deep, dark cavern.

Magic lives inside...

An image flashed in front of her closed eyes. The hilt of a sword, a flash of a smile, a fist pounding at his heart.

Morganne mimicked the gesture, thumping her own heart three times and for want of company, called out into the darkness. "Magic lives inside my heart."

Her voice bounced back to her from all directions, a symphony, a song swelling from truth. Rising to her knees, Morganne thrust her head backward, yelling, "Magic lives within my heart!"

The song louder now, like a drumming beat or galloping hooves. Somehow the thoughts, the song, brought her strength. Power pulsed through her blood and she found the strength to stagger to her feet.

Hands splayed at her sides, her fingers parted, pointing toward the depths of the earth. She called for the power from Mother Earth and the roots of the world's trees that tangled and twisted beneath the surface of the world. Head tilted back, she called to the wind and air that first rippled through her sodden curls, then whipped around her like a frenzied God. The constant *drip, drip, drip* of stagnant water started to flow —a cascading waterfall in the depth of the darkness.

Fireheart, she called unto herself.

"I am Fireheart!" Morganne yelled, and with the words upon her lips, a flickering heat raged within her heart. Sweat formed at her temples, life pulsed in her veins. And she knew now, she knew where the magic of the world resided, and it had resided inside her all along.

Morganne screamed into the darkness with every ounce of energy she possessed. She screamed for her sisters, for her mother, for poor, brave Kay, and for her horse. She screamed for Bedivere. She screamed *loudly* for Bedivere, finding extra strength in his name and heart, but mostly, Morganne screamed for herself.

And she began to glow.

Ice yellow, like the sun's own rays, burst from her heart lighting the cavern and the surrounding chasm. Her thrumming heart beat to the rhythm of galloping hooves. She looked ahead, her emerald eyes dancing like green flames, and though no ground stretched beneath her feet, she charged forward regardless.

The ground appeared as she ran, cracking and thundering together as she raced forward in her new belief, white flames shimmering in her footsteps' wake. A shimmering heat full of impossible possibilities. She made her own light as she reached the exit of the hell-hole. Her heart thrumming louder and louder with each step.

She breached the threshold, gasping at the fresh air filling her lungs, and she halted.

It was not just the sound of her heart thrumming, but Angelfire's hooves pounding the ground toward her too. And as the fire horse bounded closer, mane dancing like wildfire in the winds, it was his rider that stopped her heart.

"Bedivere!" she called, her hands clasping her flaming heart.

Angelfire reared to a stop in front of her, Bedivere slid from his back. And in one swift moment, he grabbed his witch around the waist and wrapped her in a tight embrace. Morganne sobbed, happiness and relief tied together in one overwhelming emotion.

"You knew!" she sobbed. Bedivere pulled away, wiping her tears with the pad of his thumb. He did not return her smile, his brow a knot of angst between his dark eyebrows. "What is it? What's wrong?"

Bedivere hesitated.

But it was Angelfire who spoke into her mind, a

voice she had always longed to hear. But his first words chilled her burning heart.

It's our family. She intends to kill them. All of them.

Morganne gritted her teeth. It was time to finish what she started.

22

AN EMPTY SPACE

*S*he paced a circle around the smoldering campfire, watching the smoke swirl in shapes against the wind. Sunbeams broke through the forest canopy, which did nothing to warm Emrysa's cold half-heart—for she knew the truth of things.

"I have until nightfall for my body to return."

The witch snarled, staring at the place where Bedivere had slept, nothing but an empty space now, which she felt as deeply as a freshly-dug grave the boy may as well have hand-dug for himself.

He would pay.

They all would.

Yet, with the return of her ancient form wrapping around her soul, would also bring forth her unlimited well of magic once again—not the once-used-and-gone shallow depths her host's mortal body offered. And though the thought of her cold, hard frame returning, with the thick glug of blood in her veins cramping her stomach and clenching her half-heart, she would at least be free from her incarceration. If not her curse.

For the deal was done.

The oath sealed.

And Emrysa would stop at nothing to get to the truth of things, and that started with the death of the entire Cheval family.

"Onwards," Emrysa called, staring to the touch-stone that welcomed her home.

And in an instant, she was gone, and the sun hid its face behind the clouds.

23

KILL THE WITCH

Fireheart slowed to a stilted, worried trot, tossing his head in agitation.

I must check Shadowind and Moonglow, the horse thought into Morganne's mind as he stared into the paddocks surrounding the cottage. He could not see his fellow horses and Morganne felt the panic rising in his blood.

She slid off his back, followed by Bedivere. In one heartbeat, the fire horse disappeared behind a dust storm and galloping hooves. Morganne's heart pounded to the same rhythm. Bedivere squeezed her hand.

"The blue flame has dissipated," Morganne said, though the smell of smoke and fear still lingered. "The witch kept her promise."

"Do not be so sure," Bedivere said, scouting the area. "She is as cunning as a wild fox."

Morganne nodded, then cocked her head toward her homestead in the distance. "Come on," Morganne urged, pulling away from the knight.

"Wait," he said, grabbing her. "We need to show caution. I'll check the back of the cottage first. Wait here."

Bedivere unsheathed his sword; the sound of its metallic twang grated on Morganne's bones, and he ran, sword poised, scanning his surrounds as he scurried down the hillside toward her homestead.

Morganne bit her lip; she could not wait, no matter his warning. And she took flight as Bedivere disappeared from view.

WITH HESITANT STEPS, she tiptoed into the cottage. Upon the floor, Amara looked up with dizzy confusion. She clasped her head with one hand, her forehead scrunched in pain.

"Morganne?" Amara questioned with gaping black eyes full of wonder. "We thought you were dead."

Amara scrambled to her feet, swaying, and held the wall as she staggered toward her sister, then wrapped her in a weak embrace that spoke a thousand apologies in half a breath. Amara whispered, as heavy as a brewing storm, into her sister's thick red curls. "We thought we lost you."

Light footsteps hastened toward them. Followed by heavy, slow footfalls. Fae and Mother. They threw themselves into an embrace, clutching the returned girl as if they held the pieces of the universe in their arms and wished for them not to break apart.

Fae pulled away lightly. "The blue flame…" she rubbed her forehead, her usual clear ice-blue eyes dim with a painful haze. "It only just died down. What does it mean, Morganne?"

"It means we *must* hurry, the witch Emrysa is close, and she wants revenge. She is coming here to kill us, to kill our bloodline." She cast her eyes at Mother, who clutched her throat as if she feared the words verging on escape. "We have no time for greetings or conversations. She's here, somewhere, and we must kill her, now and forever. Banishment alone is not safe enough, as I now know too well."

Mother nodded, her complexion pale and waxen, while sweat lingered on her upper lip. She had lived the history and knew the depths of Emrysa's fury. Gathering as much strength as she could muster, Mother rasped, clutching her chest and turning to Amara and

Fae. "We must combine our powers. The blue flame has held us for too long and our powers are weak. Far too weak to take on the might of Emrysa."

Amara nodded. "Agreed. Together, we may stand a chance."

The three composed themselves, gearing up for the fight. But they staggered from the room, still weak from the dark magic's grip.

"Wait."

Fae turned. "What is it, Morganne?"

"Prepare yourselves, for the witch took things from me…" she turned away, emerald eyes glassy. "She took a piece of my heart… my blood… my…"

"Dear child!" Mother cried, her fearful voice full of regret and pain. She marched to her daughter, pulling her toward her own body. "The Taking Spell." Mother spat a curse. "Damn that witch." Mother then turned to Amara and Fae. "This will be a difficult task, for the witch Emrysa will have taken Morganne's form. Her heart will beat with Morganne's blood, and the only way to reverse the spell is indeed, to kill her. Do not let her pleas for help fool you, as difficult as it may be."

Fae staggered backward. "The Killing Curse?" she clutched her heart, a small shake of her head like a whisper.

Amara nodded, folding her arms over her chest.

"We have no choice, little sister, but to end this once and for all. You saw the visions through the blue flame as I did—felt the darkness of witch Emrysa's heart. She will stop at nothing to conquer all."

"Mother?" a panicked voice cried from outside, a *familiar voice*. "Amara? Fae?"

The witches shared silent wide-eyed glances and looked through the window.

"The witch is here," Mother said, closing her eyes. Pained.

"Morganne," Amara began. "You have no magic, you must stay in here, safe, while we go outside and…" she lowered her voice to a hiss, "… *kill the witch*. I have no issues with killing her for what she's done to you, Morganne, to us." Her teeth gritted. Her dark eyes darker still.

"Where are you, oh please Goddess, say you are safe," cried the voice from outside, louder. Closer.

"Damn that witch!" cried Mother watching the imposter run toward the cottage. She clasped her hands together, forming a glowing purple light, and held it aloft ready to cast. "Come, Amara, Fae. The element of surprise is on our side, she will not suspect us to know the truth of things."

Fae clasped her hands together, silver light forming in her palms. Amara cast both arms out wide, palms facing up, clutching blackened fireballs, flickering and crackling with heat and anger.

"Morganne," Amara demanded, the protective sister. "Get back, we want no more harm coming to you while we kill this cursed witch once and for all. Go on, go!" She ushered her eldest sister backward.

Mother grabbed hold of the door handle and yanked it open with an angry determination, allowing Amara and Fae to march past, magic poised in their hands for battle. As they did, Shadow scarpered in between Mother's legs. The cat's hackles up. Its mouth opened in a hiss.

On the threshold, Mother's brows furrowed in a question and she shot a look at her returned daughter, who, in the safety of the shadows, tossed her red-golden hair over her shoulder. A sly smile broke across her face like a bloody slash. Mother paled. Eyes bulged.

This was not her daughter.

A flash of red and black light erupted outside.

"No!" Mother gasped.

But it was too late.

A macabre laugh erupted from Emrysa, dancing on the stale and smoky air as outside, the real Morganne took the force of her sisters' magic attack, and screamed.

TO THE DEATH

A black light blinded Morganne, and she flung her arms upward and around herself to block its impact. The spell deflected, booming into the dusky sky.

"No, Amara!" she cried above the crackling of dispersing magic. "It's me, your sister, *Morganne.*"

"She warned us, *witch Emrysa,*" Amara said, face of fury and thunder. Her arms a whirlwind around her body, she produced spell after spell after spell. Black sparks rained down on Morganne in relentless fury.

"Stop!" Morganne begged, weakening with her half-heart of single beat and sadness. She deflected each spell, her white-hot flame diffusing Amara's black fire into crackling dust.

"My sister is *no witch,*" Morganne said, pacing

forward, holding her gaze. She circled her hands around a fireball in her palms that grew and pulsed as she caressed her hands around it. "Fae," she ordered, "join me."

"Sisters, please," Morganne pleaded, falling to her knees.

Side-by-side, the sisters gathered their magic, silver and black swirls blending into a magic orb of power, smoke dancing around them, and the air hushed into stunned silence.

Amara began the incantation, voice rising and falling like a forgotten song unsung in eons.

"We blend our spells from fire and hell

To fill the moon with red.

Her blood will spill, the world will still,

Until the witch is dead."

Morganne crawled, her eyes darting between sisters and the empty space surrounding her. *Where is Bedivere?* He had gone around to the back of the cottage and had not returned. And where was Angelfire, for that matter? Where was *anything* that could save her? Anything that would let her sisters know they had been fooled.

Fae and Amara stalked toward her, arms trembling with the gravitas of such a heavy and dark spell.

The Killing Spell.

As if carrying the weight of the world, the sisters raised their hands above their heads, their hair glistening under the sparkling silver and black that coalesced in their hands.

Fae hesitated. "Where's Mother?" she cried over the thrum of magic.

"It doesn't matter, I've weakened the witch and now we must take her," Amara roared.

Morganne closed her eyes, fear weakening her stomach. But what could she do to change their minds? They made the choice and had believed witch Emrysa over her. From the corner of her eye, a flicker of a red cape. Her eyes darted, *Bedivere*, his dark orbs staring in disbelief and terror. And she remembered where the real magic resides.

Taking a deep breath, she rose, staring at her sisters both. She dropped her hands to her side—*and smiled.* Fae gasped, Morganne hesitated, and both turned to look at one another for half a breath, then back at their quarry. Morganne tapped her heart three times. Once for each sister to bind the triplets in love. And she cast them the *older sister look* that could belong to no-one else but the *real* Morganne. Amara's eyes widened. Fae dropped her hands to her heart, her silver smoke and flames diminishing completely.

"Sister!" Amara gasped, then turned her head back toward the cottage.

Mother screamed, serenaded by the cackling laughter of the witch, a sound belonging to the depth of hell itself.

"Oh, get on with it!" Emrysa cried, still wearing Morganne's form as she strode from the cottage in her crimson silks. With a nonchalant flick of her hand, an invisible force sent Fae crashing to the ground. She writhed, but Emrysa twisted her left hand as if turning a huge handle. Fae yelped, her wrists and ankles pinning her to the lush green grass beneath her.

With the other hand, Emrysa conjured her blue flame and smiled, cold and cruel. She threw her arm out to the middle sister, the blue light hissing through the twilight toward Amara.

Amara's eyes widened, too shocked to deflect, too slow to attack.

"NO!" screamed Morganne, as the flame hurtled toward her sister.

A flash of red. This time, Bedivere's cape as he flew at Amara, colliding into her body and slamming her to the floor with a thump. The blue flame exploded on impact upon his back. He lay still and solid over Amara's body, pinning her to the ground with his weight.

"Oh, you heroic idiot!" Emrysa said, throwing now a mocking look of pity as she shook her head at the boy who stirred so much emotion in her half heart.

Emrysa dusted her hands, which had aged and withered with the extensive magic she had cast. Emrysa did not care, for nightfall was already upon them and she would lose her form, but not her revenge.

"That's them dealt with, for now," Emrysa said. Her eyes narrowed and darkened as she glared at Morganne. The emerald green draining to the color of death. "Your family's death will come quickly, I assure you. But yours will not, your death will be a thing of endurance."

Emrysa flicked her wrist, forming a flickering whip of blue frenzy, snapping through the air. It sliced toward Morganne, its tendrils snatching. Morganne crossed her forearms over her face, deflecting the blow. Then, with its power dissipated, Morganne grappled the prongs of the whip and sent it back with a double push of her hands. She gasped at the blazing heat across her sizzling palms.

Emrysa flicked Morganne's deflective spell away with her arm, but staggered backwards with the force of it. She gritted her teeth, pressing forward, this time twirling her flame whip through the air above her head. It gathered momentum and morphed into a lasso,

pulling the world's wind into itself. Leaves whirled in its
universe, wind howled, and Emrysa's body morphed—
peeling skin, wispy hair, but her power did not dimin-
ish. Her crimson dress tattered into rags, blackness
seeping up the hem until it engulfed her completely.
The world altered beneath Morganne's feet, almost as
if the globe itself stopped and turned in the opposite
direction, following the line of the whip, following
Emrysa's spell.

Morganne gasped as the air from her lungs
exploded outward to follow the spell, her wild red hair
a tangle across her face, obscuring her view. She then
realized she was standing in the very meadow where
her magic failed her so many times. She cast those
thoughts away, and glanced at her sisters, and Bedivere
prostrate on the ground. Morganne tied her hair back
in a scruffy ponytail, stood tall and, ripping off her
cloak, she whispered secrets to the world.

And the world listened.

SISTERS OF THREE

*B*racing her hands to her side, fingers splayed toward the ground, Morganne screamed into the heavens, hauling the power of the universe back into her lungs. She raised her arms, commanded thunder, and roared as Emrysa's flickering lasso severed the air toward her. Morganne stepped *into it*, banishing its power as she flung her arms outward from her heart. Again, Emrysa staggered back, more from shock this time, her face transforming into grim determination. Morganne's features matched it, only where Emrysa's face was an explosion of hatred and rage, Morganne's was a mirror of love and hope. A powerful commodity, but was it powerful enough? Above the two battling witches, in the universe created within the circle of the lasso, storm clouds billowed into themselves, rolling and pulsing. Emrysa's dark clouds coalesced into Morganne's white clouds that fought back.

"I will not let you win," Morganne screamed.

"There is no choice, you pathetic creature." Emrysa laughed, though no smile broke her enraged features. From the space where Morganne's half-heart beat in Emrysa's chest, a blue fire surged and raged.

The next spell-war happened quicker than Morganne's eyes could perceive, yet her body moved instinctively, working with nature to fight the darkness. From hand-to-hand, Emrysa cast out flames of crimson and emerald and indigo; left hand, right hand, left hand, right hand. Morganne deflected them all, her arms twisting like a tempest around her body. A block across her body sent indigo flames crackling to the ground which sizzled, the grass dying on impact. Morganne's right arm flung upward, protecting her face and sending a green light shooting into a tree that lit in flames and smoldered. Then the crimson came for her, different to flames. Blood-laced smoke, all-encompassing and consuming, swirled around and over Morganne. Impossible to deflect.

"No!" whispered Morganne, her eyes as wide as fear herself. As it surrounded her, Emrysa's voice echoed in her mind.

You called for me, Fireheart, our souls are as one.

"Get out!" screamed Morganne. "Get out of my mind."

Emrysa cackled, full of humor and disdain.

Morganne breathed in all the love she could; from her sisters frozen and watching in awe. From Bedivere motionless on the ground. From Angelfire, who had saved her soul so many times before. And with that, the thrumming of his hooves, and more.

The horses raced to the witches, flashes of red, black, and white hurtling toward Emrysa who held a blood flame, the flame of death, in her clutches.

"With my fire of smoke and coal

I bind you now unto my soul."

Emrysa roared, flinging the flame at Morganne, too transfixed to notice the stampede careering toward her. Angelfire raced into the witch, knocking her to the floor, hooves pounding upon her body. Emrysa screamed, while Morganne turned to her sisters, and cast.

One: a flick of a hand to unpin Fae.

Two: a rise of both hands to remove Bedivere from Amara's body.

Three: a nod to both as they rose to stand.

"Combine!" Morganne urged, but Amara shook her head.

"She is too strong. We need one more, we need one more element. We are only three."

And Morganne knew her meaning immediately. Fae as soft and strong as the air and wind. Amara as grounded as the earth. Morganne herself, a Fireheart. Morganne shot a look, *where is Mother?* Emrysa staggered to her feet. Bedivere lay still on the ground. The horses circled amongst the storm and chaos.

Me, use me as your fourth element of the world, said a voice older than time and softer than meadow hay. Her eyes flickered to Angelfire, the horse stood proud now —stamping hoof, his head and neck held high, wind blowing his mane of flames.

I am a being of nature, I hold all elements within.

Morganne felt her eyes swell with salty tears, and the horse seemed to nod, as if this was his doing. Her heart swelled like a raging ocean, binding her to water and fire both. She turned to Amara and saw the fire and passion in her features, bound both to earth and fire. And Fae, beautiful, delicate Fae, holding her own like a gentle spring breeze with the power to create hurricanes and raging storms. Between them, they held the power of the world.

Sisters of three once more.

BLOOD AND BONE

*T*he three sisters and Angelfire wrapped Emrysa in a circle, each sister and horse an element for the magic to surge. They closed in on the witch, whose arms swung around her body with such complicated hand gestures, her wrists moving in such intricate and impossible ways, showing her as an unnatural being. She morphed further as the sun set, and the moon showed its face on the horizon. Her tattered black rags dissolved into a darker midnight. Her scraggy hair thickening, the ends turning black and shiny, morphing into the feathers of ravens' wings glinting in its own midnight. Her eyes glowed amber.

"You cannot take me!" she bellowed, incanting into her black thunderclouds. "No one can take me!"

Blood-colored smoke flowed around her, branching

out at the sisters and Angelfire like gnarled claws. But the sisters stood their ground. With their arms held out wide beside them, their magic flowed through one and all, connecting them and Angelfire as one, and multiplying through each connection.

"You are wrong, witch Emrysa," Morganne called. "For we are not one. We are sisters of three in heart and blood, and grounded to the world's heart."

Angelfire pounded a hoof at the turf. *Come!* He commanded his kin. And from the shadows of the spell-war, Shadowind and Moonglow stormed to join the circle.

I bind you to the power of the moon, called Moonglow. The magic surged through her as she entered the magic circle. Fae smiled at her white horse.

And I bind you to the power of night and shadows, Shadowind promised, nodding a head to Amara opposite him.

Emrysa, like a panicked wild beast, frothed at the mouth. Spittle formed at the corner of her lips. Her mouth opened impossibly wide, and she howled—a coarse sound of a raven's caw and an eagle's attacking scream bursting forth

Through the circle created by sisters and horses, magic surged. A barrier. A safe place. A connection more powerful than the most dangerous witch in history. Morganne called the spell from an ancient place within. Knowing it from her foremothers, feeling it from the earth.

"I unbind the curse that holds us true

To break the shackles tied to you

By blood and lung I call my heart

To leave your body as you depart."

The world around them inhaled. A still, eerie silence quieting the chaos. Wind dropped to a whisper, the horses' manes resting to their necks in a tangled mess. The sisters cast glances at one another. Emrysa snarled in the stillness.

Heartbeats paused.

Blood stopped.

The Universe turned away for one, brief moment.

And the circle broke, the magic of the world lost in a wilderness of faraway faerie roads. The sisters dropped their hands, shoulders hunched in anticipation. And then it came—a surge from the center of the Earth itself.

Emrysa's amber eyes widened, her beady, black pupils flickering from one sister to the next. Slowly, she lifted her arms, and the sisters crouched into a defensive stance—hands poised for attack, anticipating the witch's onslaught in the sinister silence and power surging through the air. Emrysa stepped forward and roared, shaking the very ground beneath their feet. But with the instinct of sisters of blood and bone, Morganne, Amara, and Fae roared louder. They threw their hands toward the witch, the entire magic of the universe surging from the center of the earth through their feet, anchoring them to the roots of the world's trees. Anchoring them to the universe as the world spun faster and faster, a blur of colors and chaos.

A raven cawed.

Horses shrieked, and Morganne found all the fire in her heart to command the spell on her lips, and her magic surged from her toward Emrysa.

The witch screamed, howling at the rising moon, as red and black smoke caused a whirlwind around her— blood and darkness as one. It surged upward and outward, taking with it black feathers and deathly screams.

"You'll never take me!" Emrysa screamed, yet her voice weakened and croaked on the dying wind.

An explosion of color and sound erupted.

Horses scattered.

Sisters fell.

Thunder diminished.

And Emrysa was gone.

A NEW VIEW

*A*ngelfire pawed the ground where the dark witch had stood, but nothing was left of Emrysa other than her midnight gowns and a flurry of raven's feathers.

"You did it!" Fae sang in a joyful tune of disbelief. She ran to Morganne, who stared at her own hands, mesmerized by the power pulsing at her fingertips. She laughed as Fae wrapped her in an embrace and caught eyes with Amara from over her younger sister's shoulder.

Amara nodded, serious as thunder, and started to speak. Morganne shook her head to silence her. There was no need for apologies from her middle sister, for Amara had been right all along. The chaos that had been caused belonged to Morganne, all apologies were hers.

Morganne untangled herself from Fae's embrace, and with timid steps, made her way to Bedivere. She clasped her chest and, holding her breath, knelt beside the boy. Her hand hovered before touching him, fearing his cold skin against her fingers.

"Bedivere?" she whispered. Silence, except for her thudding half-heart beating against her chest. Had she not been so concerned about the knight, she may have noticed that strange single beat was still incomplete.

"He will be okay," croaked a weak voice behind her. "It seems the witch had *some heart* after all and only used a Dazing Spell for the boy."

"Mother!" Morganne cried, torn between a need to embrace her, and a fear from her mother's wrath.

After all I have put them through.

Mother trembled, her face aged decades in the few days the blue flame held her. A rare smile broke across her face, her hard eyes softened, glistening with tears. She grabbed Morganne, pulling her to her feet and hugging her with the fierceness only produced by maternal love.

"I am so proud of you, my girl," Mother whispered into Morganne's ear through her mass of thick red curls.

Morganne suppressed her urge to cry. "I'm sorry I started all of this, Mother," Morganne said, voice aquiver.

"Shh," Mother said. "You were always destined for great things, it was foretold."

Morganne pulled away. "Foretold? But I thought you didn't believe in me? I thought I was a disappointment because I could not wield magic like my sisters."

Mother tightened her lips and turned away, lest her daughter see her tears. "I was never disappointed with you, Fireheart. If anything, I feared you. I feared the magic I knew you were capable of wielding—"

"*Fireheart?*" Morganne questioned, stepping back. "How did you know Emrysa's name for me?"

"Mother?" Amara asked as she stepped toward them. "What are you hiding from us?"

Fae, quiet as always, said not a word, but her intense ice-blue eyes bore into her mother's mind, trying to decipher her thoughts.

Mother fumbled with her fingers, sniffed, then pushed her shoulders back. "There is a lot you do not know, but so much has been foretold." She turned to Morganne. "It was written in the wind that my first born would bring forth and battle the Dark One. That was why I panicked and struck out at you when you found the book. I feared you would bring her back into the world before you were strong enough to fight her. I feared I would lose you—"

"Then why keep that knowledge from me! It was my knowledge, that information belonged to me!" Morganne spat.

Amara sucked air between her clenched teeth. Fae stared in disbelief.

Mother shook her head. "No, daughter, it was my burden to bear. It will not do to foretell your own fate— destiny is a path you must walk alone. And I have a great deal more burdens chewing at my soul and hardening my heart. But they *are* mine to bear. Yet, your power *has* surprised me, and for that, the future suddenly holds more hope."

Morganne fought her older-sister instinct to reprimand, and wondered if she was suddenly grasping the edges of her mother's harshness, her constant urgency and seriousness. Her mother was not bitter, but pained, and this knowledge softened Morganne's half-beat-heart. She reached for her mother's hand, and Mother took it with a tender squeeze.

They smiled, and somehow it bonded them more than any binding spell could achieve.

"Morganne?" A soft slur of a voice said from her feet. "I can see right up your skirts."

Morganne gasped, blushed, and stepped away from

Bedivere lying on the ground beneath her. With a curious mixture of outrage and relief, Morganne stared at her sisters and Mother in turn, then down at Bedivere whose lazy smile lit up the darkening evening. And in half a heartbeat, each and every one of them burst out laughing. A tinkle that danced on the evening breeze with the soft, contented sound of relaxed horses grazing under the moon.

EPILOGUE

3 Days Later...

"There is not a single finding spell under the moon that has worked," Mother said. "For all intended purposes, Emrysa is no longer here."

Amara rolled her eyes. "Well, we know she is not *here.*" She slapped her hands on the wooden table.

"Yes, but I mean *here*...in *this* world."

"You do not believe her to be dead?" Morganne asked, and mother shook her head.

"She is neither dead, my child," Mother continued. "For no summoning spirit spell has worked either."

"Which means?" Morganne pressed, tired of incantations, tired of spells. Tired of *not* finding out what really happened to Emrysa when she disappeared.

"It means I must leave." Mother looked at her hands, then a jug half empty of water, then the fingernail of her thumb. Anything not to catch eyes. Anything but tell the truth.

"Mother?" Fae pressed.

A heavy sigh.

"I need to reform the old coven, I need to find the bloodlines of the original witches who helped defeat witch Emrysa in the beginning," Mother said. Shadow, the black cat purred, and wrapped his body around her legs.

"And we can't come with you," Fae filled in the gaps from her mother's grave tone.

Amara rose from her chair, flattening down her gown. "You can't expect us to sit around here and wait for you."

"No," Mother said, she straightened her back and puffed out her chest, bracing herself. "We cannot stay here. This home is her touchstone—" she glanced at Morganne who cast her eyes downward. "I have arranged for your father to collect you. He will be here upon the hour."

"*Father?!*" Both Amara and Morganne spat together. Even Fae's soft feature's crumpled into confusion that bordered on curiosity.

"We haven't seen that man since I can even remember, since before we could *talk!*" Amara shouted. "What right does he have to come back into our lives now?"

Mother pressed her hands forward blocking Amara's bitter words. "It wasn't a decision I took lightly, Amara. But for all his irreparable traits, the man is a world-renowned alchemist, and you are sure to learn from him in my absence—"

"Pfft, *learn* from him?" Amara said. "What? Learn how to desert family? Learn how to not give a horse's arse about anyone else but ourselves?"

"Amara!" Mother chastised. "This is not up for debate. This is what's happening. Now, pack your clothes."

Without a whisper, Fae followed her mother's orders and her curiosity, which far outweighed her anger or frustration. Besides, who knew what she could learn about the ancient art form of alchemy.

"I'm not going," Amara said, defiant, and turned to Morganne, widening her eyes. "Tell her," Amara whispered.

A rap on the door, and Morganne spun, knowing who to expect.

Bedivere slid in, grimacing with the tension hovering in the air. Morganne smiled. Amara bristled at his presence.

"So, I'm, er, I'm ready. I must make haste back to

Camelot." He turned to Morganne, holding out his hand. Amara watched their fingers entwine. "Thank you, Witch Cheval for aiding me in my recovery. But it's time Morganne and I leave."

"You're leaving? With *him?*" Mother asked, incredulous.

"I am no longer a child, Mother," Morganne said.

Mother nodded with a knowing smirk. Her daughter would *always* be her child in her eyes.

"There is much we can gather from Camelot, Witch Cheval," Bedivere said to Mother. "Kay was affected by the witch, he may have insights. And the king has other means to gather intelligence."

"Yes, I have heard," Mother said, thoughtful, staring into the distance. "The king has a magician, Merlin, is that right?"

"One and the same," Bedivere said with a lopsided grin that matched Mother's.

She giggled like a schoolchild with a secret causing all daughters to stare. Amara took the opportunity and stepped forward.

"Well, I'll go too, to Camelot. If Fae is happy to learn from the man who calls himself our father, I'll be happy learning from this king's magician, Manning, or whatever you said his name was."

Bedivere hesitated, repressing a smirk that would

not go away. He covered his mouth with his hand then rubbed his cheeks. Failing to hide his amusement, he looked away.

"What?" Amara hissed. "Mother is off to reform her jolly old coven, Fae can go and learn how to turn coal into obsidian with that stupid man, and *I* shall learn from the king's great magician."

Bedivere shook his head, and Amara scowled at his humor, the way his perfect lips curled up at the sides. She watched those lips intently as he spoke. "Merlin, is, well—"

"—Unusual," Mother finished for Bedivere.

"That's one word for him," Bedivere chuckled and Mother continued.

"—Cantankerous, arrogant, shameless, and brilliant would be more."

"You already seem to share traits, Amara, although the only brilliance I can vouch for is your brilliant mood swings," Bedivere joked, and all sisters scowled at him. Even Morganne dug him in the ribs.

"What?!" he laughed, then very abruptly, stopped.

"I consent," Mother said, softening to Bedivere. "Morganne and Amara, you'll go to Camelot to see if Merlin can help locate Emrysa—"

"I didn't need permission," Amara said under her breath, which Mother ignored.

"And Fae... where did that girl get to? Fae?" Mother called.

Like a summer breeze, Fae walked from her bedroom, a small cloth bag packed with her belongings in her hand. She defused the air from tension with her smile.

"Father is here," Fae said.

Outside, a grand ornate carriage arrived, pulled by six glamorous dapple-gray horses with large feather plumes at their head. The horses came to a stand-still and a lithe man jumped out, full of spring and mischief.

"Drat it," Mother cursed as she watched her estranged husband skip up the garden path. She cocked her head to better see him from the window and without missing a beat clicked her fingers, transforming into the young woman she used to be.

"Witch Cheval," Bedivere said with a long slow whistle. "I can see where your daughters get their stunningly good looks from."

It was Amara who smiled the most at this, her eyes dashing away when they caught Bedivere's. Morganne was too busy watching her father outside the window to notice.

The cottage door burst open. And just like that, the

gray-haired man seemed to fill the room with his presence.

"Ah! There you are," the man said glancing at Morganne, Amara, and Fae in turn. He twiddled his immaculately-groomed mustache that curled up at the ends. "Look at that, the three S's. Sullen. Serious. And —" he eyed Fae, "Oh! And Secretive, it would seem."

Fae looked to her feet.

The man noticed the bag in her hand, made an equation, and knew the truth of it.

"So it looks like it's just you and me. Come on, Offspring," he called over his shoulder to Fae as he walked out. He hesitated with the dramatic flair of an amateur theater performer. Then turned to Mother with a charming smile. "You look divine, my little trinket, as always. Remember, my offer still stands."

Mother blushed.

"Come on, Offspring. Chippy chop. It's now or never." And he waltzed from the door to his carriage.

"I…" Fae hesitated, feeling the heaviness of good-byes in her heart.

IN A FLURRY of tears and embraces, Fae climbed aboard the gold-gilded carriage—her slender fingers tracing the intricate shapes within the gold that looked like wings. She stared out as her home shrank in the distance, pressing her hand to the window as she passed the paddocks and meadows where her horse Moonglow grazed.

I had no time to say goodbye, she called out to her mind. And Moonglow raised her head as the carriage passed.

Fear not, for we shall meet again, Moonglow said with a toss of her elegant mane.

"Oh! Don't be so sullen child!" her father said with, somehow, not a hint of chiding. "Look here…" he pulled out a small silver hand mirror. "You just whisper what you want to see and it will appear in the mirror. A jolly good bit of alchemy that, simple as it is. Anyway, it'll keep that little ice-heart of yours from freezing over when we're at Castell Draig."

"Castell Draig?" Fae asked, taking the pretty mirror to her palm and opening the lid. "*Home,*" she whispered, already feeling her heart ache with the absence of her sisters.

"Yes, Celtic for Dragon Castle—your new home. It is said it was built on the legends of dragons. Or built on the bones of dragons. I can never remember which." Father chortled lightly.

But Fae wasn't listening because home did indeed shimmer into life in the mirror. And in that mirror, she saw Morganne staring into her own reflection in the river, her forehead creased with concern.

"Closer," Fae whispered, holding the magic contraption to her face and watched in horror as she understood her sister's worry. Upon Morganne's collarbone was a mark, not yet fully formed, but its eerie glow was there all the same, and it looked just like two crescent moons back to back.

The sign of the necromancers.

Emrysa may have gone, but she left her mark.

Fae spun to face her father. "Father, what do you know of black magic?" Fae asked, her words tumbling from her mouth like lava.

He turned to her with confusion written across his aged, yet handsome face. "Dark magic?" he asked with the look of alarm, before his face broke into a delightful, charming smile. "Everything, dear Offspring. Everything."

Fae found herself smiling along with him.

Good, she thought with a nod, then turned her attention to the rolling countryside toward the dragon castle awaiting her.

End of Episode 2

Follow Fae as she discovers there are darker things than secrets, but can she handle the truth?

Find out in the fast paced and electrifying Episode 3 of Dragon Heart.

Want to stay up to date with all things Magic and Mage? Scan the code below to sign up to my Readers Newsletter and get your hands on a special Witch Hearts inspired Swag Bag full of exclusive gifts and freebies.

DRAGON HEART

When the moon-marked are called, the darkness will follow...

he evil witch Emrysa is gathering strength to summon her Dark Army to life, and the Cheval sisters must find a way to thwart her once and for all.

But while Morganne and Amara study dark magic with the king's magician in Camelot, Fae discovers darker secrets hidden beneath an alchemist's castle built on lies and deceit—a secret that will bring her closer to the evil witch than she ever anticipated.

But with the evil army rising, the darkness descending, and the moon-marked morphing into otherworldly beings, Fae needs to do more than learn the art of alchemy to help protect the people of Camelot.

She needs to learn how to open portals into other worlds, enlist help from ancient magical beings, and allow her dragon heart to roar.

There are darker things than secrets, but can Fae handle the truth?

Find out in the fast paced and electrifying Episode 3 of Dragon Heart.

ABOUT THE AUTHOR

Angharad Thompson Rees is a multi passionate creative with a Little Whimsey. A screenwriter, comic scriptwriter, poet, illustrator, and author of fantasy novels and creative journals for children and young adults. Weaving strong imagery with poetical prose, Angharad's stories capture the imagination of young and old with her whimsical offerings.

Discover out more at:
www.littlewhimsey.com

ALSO BY ANGHARAD THOMPSON REES

Teens

Witch Hearts

Fire Heart

Dragon Heart

Raven Heart

Middle Grade Adventures

Forever Night

The Snow Pony

Magical Adventures & Pony Tales

The Painted Pony

The Galloping Pony

The Girl and her Pony

The Runaway Pony

The Desert Pony

The Wooden Pony

Made in the USA
Las Vegas, NV
27 October 2024

10540317R00104